WHEN MIDNIGHT COMES...

by CAROL BEACH YORK

Cover illustration by Lydia Rosier

SCHOLASTIC BOOK SERVICES

NEW YORK • TORONTO • LONDON • AUCKLAND • SYDNEY • TOKYO

To Carol Farley
dear friend and fellow writer

ISBN 0-590-31820-9

12 11 10 9 8 7 6 5 4 3 2   0 1 2 3 4 5/8

Printed in the U. S.A.   06

WHEN
MIDNIGHT
COMES...

1

Mrs. Bridgeport was alone in the gray light of a late-winter afternoon. She had just come home. No lamps were lit, and the fading hours gave the house an eerie gloom. Polished living-room tables glimmered in the dusk.

She was a beautiful woman — slender, dark-haired, fashionably dressed, moving with an easy grace to lay her coat across the arm of a chair and switch on a table lamp.

As she lit the fire in the fireplace, a small white cat on the sofa stirred from sleep and blinked at the flames.

Above the mantel the children gazed out from a large oil portrait: demure little Emily; Charles holding an open book; Joan with her lovely long-lashed eyes.

Restlessly Mrs. Bridgeport moved about the room, turning on more lamps. Her club meeting had been over earlier than she expected. She could have gone to meet the bus after all. But that would probably have disappointed Joan, who was so proud of her new driver's license, always so eager to do errands in the car.

"But it's perfect, Mother," Joan had exclaimed. "I have early classes Thursday. *I'll* meet the bus."

Joan would be coming soon. . . Mrs. Bridgeport stood by her writing desk and absentmindedly straightened an ivory letter opener, a pen, a box of stationery. The calendar pad had not been changed, and she tore off the top page, noting that it was the first of March.

"March is the month my mother was really afraid of," John Steinbeck wrote in *Journal of a Novel.* "She practically held her breath until it was over every year. For everything bad happened to our family in March."

Mrs. Bridgeport sighed and crumpled the last day of February in her slim fingers.

"March is a nervous month, neither winter nor spring, and the winds make people nervous."

Mrs. Bridgeport agreed with that. She hated March. Neither winter nor spring . . . a dreary time of cruel winds and cold rains and dark afternoons.

She did not know how long she had been sitting on the sofa, stroking the white cat, when gradually she became aware of a sound coming softly through the silent house.

It was the sound of a clock ticking where there had been no sound before.

Mrs. Bridgeport turned and looked toward the living-room doorway and the hall beyond. Stairs led up from the hall to a landing where a grandfather clock stood. Surely it could not be the grandfather clock. It had not run for months.

But she was almost immediately distracted by the sound of the front door opening, footsteps in the hall, and Joan's voice calling, "Mother? Are you home?"

Mrs. Bridgeport set the cat aside and adjusted her face into an expression of pleasure and welcome she did not feel.

Why don't you send Wilma to spend a few weeks with us? she had written in reply to her sister Catherine's unhappy letter. Almost at once she had regretted the impulsive invitation, but it was too late then. She could not call back her words. The invitation had been written and sent. And now Wilma was here.

"Mother — " Joan appeared in the living-room doorway, drawing Wilma along beside her, and Mrs. Bridgeport rose to greet them.

Although she had not seen her sister's child for several years, Wilma was much as Mrs. Bridgeport remembered her. Overweight. Cheap, ill-fitting clothes. Drab, stringy hair. Weak eyes behind thick glasses. Mrs. Bridgeport had never really liked her.

"Hello, Aunt Madeleine."

And because she was sorry to see Wilma and she could not do anything about it now, Mrs. Bridgeport said as cheerfully as she could:

"Wilma — we're so glad you could come."

2

The younger children returned from school through the darkening afternoon.

Emily was first, in a red coat and buckled shoes. A fine, misty rain had begun just as she came, and raindrops shone on her soft brown hair. She stood shyly by her mother's chair in the living room, eyes downcast.

"You remember Wilma," Mrs. Bridgeport said encouragingly.

Emily kept her eyes down. She was only eight years old, and she did not remember her cousin Wilma at all.

Charles came running in next, dumping his books on the hall table, eager to tell his mother how much Teacher had liked his science notebook. He had forgotten today was the day Wilma was coming.

"Charles, you remember your cousin Wilma."

Charles stared as blankly as Emily had.

"Charles usually comes in with a great rush," Mrs. Bridgeport explained lightly. She wished Wilma would say something; instead of sitting there like a lump.

Joan was perched on the arm of the sofa. "I've never been on a long bus trip," she said companionably. "I bet it was fun."

"It was okay."

"Anna's home." Emily leaned closer against her mother's chair.

Mrs. Bridgeport listened a moment. She could hear water runing in the kitchen sink, a cupboard door closing. "You're right, sweetie." She smoothed Emily's hair and turned to Wilma. "Anna's our new housekeeper. We don't have Sophie anymore. Do you remember Sophie, who was here when you were a little girl? She got married and left. Anna's been here about two years. She's really wonderful."

"Wait till you taste her cooking," Joan said.

Then the conversation ground to a halt again.

"Well, isn't it nice to have Wilma visiting us." Mrs. Bridgeport smiled around at everyone, and her eyes met Joan's. Joan was the only one of the children who knew about Aunt Catherine's letter, and why Wilma had come.

I just don't know what to do about Wilma, Catherine had written. *Since she quit school in October she hasn't been able to find a job. She tried at first, but now I think she's too discouraged to bother. And of course John is still upset about her quitting school. He hardly speaks to her. I can't tell you how miserable everything is....*

The letter had aroused Mrs. Bridgeport's sympathy; it had also quickened her sense of gratitude for the blessings she had. Even though she was a widow, she had a beautiful home and enough money to live a very pleasant life and to buy her children everything they needed. And her children were the delight of her life. Charles, even at ten, was showing signs of outstanding scholarship at school. Emily was as sweet and lovable as the little white cat that slept on the sofa cushion. Joan was one of the most beautiful and popular girls at Greencourt High School.

"It's too bad Wilma didn't keep on somehow until she graduated," Mrs. Bridgeport had said, sharing the letter with Joan the day it arrived. "She had only one more year to go."

"Why did she quit?" Joan loved high school. The idea that anybody should want to quit amazed her.

"She never was much of a student," Mrs. Bridgeport answered vaguely. "And I guess she didn't have many friends at school."

There had been an earlier letter, in October, when Wilma quit school. Mrs. Bridgeport had not mentioned this letter at the time, hoping that Wilma would go back to school and everything would work out, after all. But it hadn't.

Joan looked sober. "No, I guess school wouldn't be much fun if you didn't have friends. Well, how come she can't get a job?"

Mrs. Bridgeport smiled to herself at Joan's naïveté. Joan was so smart and pretty she would probably be hired by the first employer she met. But a school dropout with no training in anything, a dumpy, listless girl; well, chances were poor.

"She's not trained to do anything." Mrs. Bridgeport folded the letter. "I suppose she could clerk in a store or something." Her voice lacked conviction. Store clerks should have an alert, attractive appearance.

"I thought I'd write and invite Wilma to come here for a few weeks. It would be a change for her, perhaps pick up her spirits. She seemed to like it when she was here as a little girl. And it might help, to get her out of her own house for a while — be sort of a change for everybody concerned."

"But that's mean of Uncle John, to still be mad at her."

Mrs. Bridgeport patted Joan's hand. "He's disappointed that she didn't graduate."

"If Daddy were alive, would he be mad at me if I quit high school?" Joan was curious.

Her memories of her father were of a kindly, laughing man. She wouldn't ever want to quit high school, of course. But what if she had?

Mrs. Bridgeport flourished her hand to indicate that she did not answer foolish questions. Joan would never quit school.

"What do you think? Shall we invite Wilma for a visit? She'd have to share your room."

"That's no problem," Joan said. "Sure, go ahead and ask her."

Mrs. Bridgeport had felt like a good Samaritan, writing to invite Wilma, but now that Wilma had actually come, she felt her pangs of regret growing even stronger. What would she *do* with the girl, blinking behind her glasses, not saying two words? The days of the visit stretched endlessly ahead.

Mrs. Bridgeport felt guilty about her feelings, but she could not seem to help them.

There had to be a rearrangement of chairs at the dining-room table that evening. Mrs. Bridgeport always sat at the head of the table, and Joan sat at the opposite end. Emily and Charles sat at the sides. Now that Wilma was here, Emily's place was set closer to her mother's, and room was made for Wilma on Emily's side of the table.

Wilma picked at her food self-consciously. Everything was so beautiful: the lace tablecloth and the bowl of flowers, the dinner plates with a rim of roses. At the head of the table Aunt Madeleine looked like a fashion model in her lavender dress and gold bracelets.

There was even a maid in the kitchen.

It was the "mansion" Wilma remembered from childhood days. And now she had returned. But it was different now, because she was older. When she had visited as a child, she had seen only all the wonderful, beautiful things. Now she also saw herself among these beautiful things, and the dress she had chosen to wear this first night — her best — was *ugly*. *She* was ugly . . . standing in the bus station with her two old suitcases, as Joan drove up in that gorgeous car.

"I got an *A* on the notebook, Mama," Charles said, but Mrs. Bridgeport only smiled and quickly changed the subject. She hoped Wilma had not heard. Wilma had never done well in school, and Mrs. Bridgeport didn't want to talk too much about Charles's school successes in front of her.

Oh, if only everyone could be happy and beautiful and successful.

"What's dessert?" Emily asked softly, putting her head to one side and looking at her mother with dreamy eyes.

* * *

In the kitchen plump Anna was feeding the white cat.

"What's the matter with you?" she nodded, as the cat left the food untouched and padded around the room.

Anna watched suspiciously as she scooped ice cream into china saucers. At last the cat stopped and stood motionless, listening. Light glowed in the amber eyes. Then it began to move again, pacing the room.

On the kitchen windows droplets of rain glistened in the dark. Anna didn't like rainy, misty nights: She always felt there was something outside in the rain and mist, something trying to get in at her from the darkness.

Rain continued to fall through the starless night. Haze circled the streetlamps along Windsor Drive, and cars went by with a soft swish of tires on the wet paving.

At eight o'clock Emily sat obediently in the chair by Joan's dressing table, having her hair curled for the night. As gently as she could, Joan drew the comb through the long, fine hair, which somehow always got so tangled by the end of the day. A cast-off hair ribbon drooped on the edge of Emily's knee, and a pink tin box holding pink rubber curlers lay open on the table.

Wilma's suitcases in a corner of the room were a reminder that things were not quite as usual.

"I don't think she's very pretty," Emily said with tender disappointment.

Joan took a roller and twined up a section of hair. "Emmy" — she lowered her voice — "that's not a very nice thing to say."

"Do *you* think she's pretty?" Emily looked at Joan's mirror reflection above the dressing table.

"People can't help what they look like."

Emily dangled her feet and picked at the hair ribbon.

Joan was not sure how much she would say. Emily didn't know that Wilma was too poor to buy better clothes, and not smart enough to do her schoolwork. Emily didn't know Wilma had quit school because she didn't have any friends. Maybe I can transform her, Joan thought. A diet and a new hairstyle —

"Why is she visiting us?" Emily interrupted Joan's thoughts.

"Just for fun."

Joan took another pink roller and another section of hair. Her mother had said there was no need for the little ones to know about Wilma's "trouble."

Charles came lagging into the room and sank dejectedly onto the edge of Joan's bed.

"What's the matter with you?" Joan glanced over her shoulder.

Charles looked at her for sympathy. "I thought I'd get to stay up later, 'cause we have company."

"But you have to go to school in the morning. You need your sleep."

"I can stay up. I don't need any sleep. I can stay up all night."

"You'd be pretty sleepy in the morning."

"I would not."

Rain dripped at the windows.

Joan wound up another curler and looked at Charles again. "What's Wilma doing?"

Charles shrugged to show he didn't care. He wanted to stay up all night. "Calling her mother."

"That's nice," Joan said cheerfully. "Now Aunt Catherine will know she got here okay."

Charles kicked the floor with his shoe.

Joan was finished with Emily's hair, and she shooed both children out of her room. "Go on — scat."

"I could stay up *two* whole nights and I wouldn't be sleepy," Charles called back.

It wasn't long before Wilma came up, shuffling behind Mrs. Bridgeport on the deep-carpeted stairs. Emily, in a long blue flannel nightgown, her head bobbing with pink rollers, peeked from her bedroom door to say good night. On her bed the little white cat played with yesterday's hair ribbon.

"Into bed, into bed." Mrs. Bridgeport swatted Charles playfully. He called out once more to tell Joan he could stay up *three* whole nights and not be sleepy. He was giggling now, enjoying the game.

Joan helped Wilma put her things in the closet and bureau drawers. She tried to make conversation as she laid out her clothes for school the next day. But it wasn't easy.

Wilma looked around the room now and then as she hung up her skimpy wardrobe, and it was hard for Joan to tell what she was thinking. Joan's girl friends would have cried, "Oh, I love your new bedspread," or "Hey, can I try this perfume?" But Wilma only said, "You have a nice room." She might have been saying, "Please pass the bread."

"Make yourself at home." Joan motioned generously. "It's your room too while you're here."

Wilma moved closer to the dressing table. Pictures of Joan's friends were stuck in the mirror frame.

"Is this your boyfriend?"

"Oh, not particularly," Joan laughed.

Wilma lifted a small framed picture and stared at it intently. She didn't say, "Oh, he's cute." She didn't say anything. Joan hunted for words — and said the wrong ones. "That was taken at the Christmas dance."

Right away she was sorry she'd said that. Wilma had probably never been to a school dance, never worn a long party dress. She'd probably never even had a date.

Joan felt uncomfortable, afraid to say anything more lest it be the wrong thing again. Having Wilma visit wasn't turning out to be exactly what she had expected. It wasn't like having her girl friends stay overnight. That was so much *fun*. They laughed and giggled and talked about their boyfriends and polished their fingernails. But Wilma couldn't ever seem to think of anything to say.

At last Joan said, "Do you miss school?"

Wilma put the picture down. "No, I hated school."

After that Joan didn't try to talk anymore. She was glad when her mother came in for a few minutes. It was better than being alone with Wilma — at least now. By and by they would get to be friends, but now Joan felt only tired and let down. Tomorrow she would think some more about making Wilma beautiful.

Wilma lay awake long after Joan had gone to sleep. She thought of the beautiful table at dinner, the whole beautiful house. She thought of the pictures on Joan's dressing table. Pictures of friends. Wilma had no friends at home to think of now, or miss. Johnny, perhaps . . . but he had never noticed her. She was fat and ugly. She wasn't part of the "crowd." What would she have said to Johnny if he had ever really spoken to her? Well, once he had. . . *"Hey, you dropped this."* He was holding a smudged math paper, branded with a failing grade. She had taken it, awkwardly shifting her books, staring at her shoes.

She had never had a boy's picture in her bedroom. Only Johnny's image in her mind.

Wilma stared into the darkness. Joan Bridgeport had *everything*. Everything anybody could want.

And she could probably *do* everything she wanted to do. Wilma couldn't even quit school when she wanted to. Not without a battle, anyway. She could still hear the thud of her father's fist as he struck the table. *"This is nonsense. I will not have it!"* But he had had to have it. She had screamed back at him, her face flushed, her heart racing. She was friendless and ugly and dumb and she hated school and she was never going back, never, never, *never*.

Her little brothers and sisters had stared with frightened eyes at so much screaming and yelling, while her mother hovered at the edges of the commotion. "John, John — Wilma, Wilma." she kept saying, but no one listened to her.

"I hate you!" Wilma had screamed at her father — Wilma who was always so quiet you hardly knew she was around. She had run away and slammed her bedroom door. There were no pictures of boys there, no pretty clothes laid out for the next day. There was only cheap furniture crowded into a too-small room, and a younger sister's gym suit in a heap on the bed.

She had locked the door and stood kicking at it as hard as she could. She was not even aware that her father was pounding from the other side, demanding that she open it. She could only hear her own sobs and her own kicks at the door.

She had wanted to kick harder and harder and harder, until the whole world heard.

4

The morning was dark, the hall and stairs deep with shadow as Wilma came down. Emily seemed suddenly to appear out of the gloom, holding the white cat.

"See, Kitty has no claws," the little girl said solemnly, lifting the cat closer to Wilma. She studied Wilma's face to see what Wilma would think.

Wilma lifted one of the cat's paws and rubbed her thumb against the soft pink pad.

Emily had found the white cat herself and brought it home. She had found it behind a bush in the garden one summer day, like a gift left by the fairies.

"I found her, and she hasn't got any claws. Mama says someone who had her before had her claws taken off. We can't ever let her go out."

Emily caressed the cat, and her long dark hair fell forward, hiding her small face.

"Mama says if she was outside a dog might chase her and she couldn't climb a tree to get away." Emily's voice was mournful. "She couldn't fight back. Maybe the dog would eat her up."

Wilma blinked behind the thick glasses. The cat's fur was deep and silky; her fingers became lost inside.

But the cat sprang away when she touched it and disappeared down the stairs.

"Did you ever have a kitty?" Emily asked.

"No."

Emily thought about that for a moment.

"Did you ever have a puppy?"

"No," Wilma said. "I never had any pets."

"Charles has a turtle." Emily's eyes were luminous in the shadowy dusk of the stairs.

Beyond the windows a damp mist pressed close about the house. From the dining room below came the muffled sound of Charles's and Joan's voices. More faintly, from the kitchen, a teakettle whistled.

Anna turned off the gas flame, and the whistle faded to silence. Her eyes lifted again to the clock above the stove. Surely it was time for Mrs. Bridgeport to be down. Yes. With relief Anna heard the familiar voice in the dining room.

"I hope you slept well, Wilma. . . ."

Anna knew Mrs. Bridgeport would come to the kitchen in a moment, but she could not wait. Her mouth pinched, the housekeeper plodded to the door and pushed it ajar.

Mrs. Bridgeport stood beside the dining-room table, bending to kiss the top of Joan's head. Her blue morning robe fell straight from her shoulders to the floor, concealing, until she moved, elegant gold slippers.

"Can I see you, Mrs. Bridgeport?"

Mrs. Bridgeport turned and the blue robe swirled gently.

"Good morning, Anna. Yes, of course." She came toward the kitchen door, patting Emily, who had just slipped into her chair at the table.

Anna had withdrawn back into the kitchen, and Mrs. Bridgeport's gold slippers made a clicking sound on the brightly polished floor.

"Yes, Anna? What is it?"

Anna hardly needed to lift her hand to point. As soon as Mrs. Bridgeport stepped into the kitchen, the door silently swinging shut behind her, she could see for herself.

The three begonias Anna tended on the kitchen windowsill lay on the floor in a confusion of broken clay pots and scattered dirt. Anna had spread newspapers and begun to rescue what she could from the wreckage.

"Why — why — what *happened*?" Mrs. Bridgeport stopped short, her mouth open with surprise.

"It was just this way when I came in this morning." Anna motioned toward the door of her room, which adjoined the kitchen. It was a small servant's room furnished with a maple bed and dresser and an upholstered chair. In the room were also books on the occult, the spirit world, ancient superstitions from the middle-European country where Anna had grown up. But the books were secret, hidden under her bed. Only her friend Mrs. Cardalla knew about them.

Mrs. Bridgeport lifted the trailing hem of her robe as she stepped closer to the debris on the floor. She shook her head in bewilderment. The white cat did sometimes spring up on tabletops and windowsills. But she had never broken anything.

She knelt and picked at a fragment of clay pot. Then she straightened up, holding her robe so it would not brush through the dirt.

"It must have been Kitty."

Anna looked doubtful. "She sleeps upstairs."

"She must have come down," Mrs. Bridgeport said. She could not think of any other explanation.

"Such a mess," Anna said glumily.

Tiny pink blossoms had bloomed on the begonias only this week. How pretty they had looked, blooming in a row on the kitchen sill.

"I'm sure there are some more pots in the basement," Mrs. Bridgeport said. "Perhaps the plants haven't been hurt too much."

A voice from the dining room called,

"Mama," and Mrs. Bridgeport sighed. She had errands to do that day, and already the rain was beginning again.

Was that all it ever did in March, rain?

Even under the bright kitchen lights, the gloom of the day seeped in everywhere.

Besides that, Charles looked flushed this morning. She felt his forehead. Charles was never sick. Was he coming down with a cold?

Rain, rain, go away.

And what would she do with Wilma all day?

5

But somehow, slowly, the hours of the day crept by.

At two o'clock Mrs. Bridgeport sat under the shining crystal chandeliers of an uptown restaurant, drew off her gloves, laid them neatly beside her place, and, for the first time since morning, relaxed.

She had accomplished all her errands. The rain had let up at last. And she had solved the problem of what to do with Wilma by bringing her along. Between errands, Mrs. Bridgeport had shown Wilma the new Greencourt Library, City Hall, and the statue of George

Washington glistening with rain in the chill morning.

They had driven by the grade school where Emily and Charles were tucked away somewhere behind rain-streaked windows.

They had driven past the high school Joan attended.

It was not the best day for sightseeing, but Mrs. Bridgeport had been at a loss for anything else with which to entertain Wilma. The next day, Saturday, would be better, Mrs. Bridgeport consoled herself. The children would be home from school. Perhaps they could take Wilma to a movie.

"Do you like movies, Wilma?"

"Sure."

Joan and Charles and Emily always had so much to say. Mrs. Bridgeport fiddled with her gloves. She was acutely aware of ambivalent feelings — sympathy for her sister's child, and irritation at the girl's dullness. Besides having nothing to say, Wilma looked awkward and ill at ease. She sat slumped forward with her arms on the table, as though she were leaning on a sandwich-shop counter.

Mrs. Bridgeport tried not to look at her, letting her gaze wander toward the front of the restaurant, where shafts of delicately tinted light came through tall stained-glass windows. Waitresses moved between the tables, and a Strauss waltz filled the room with the romance of Old Vienna.

Mrs. Bridgeport sipped ice water and studied the menu.

When they had ordered, she settled back, resting her arms gracefully on the red velvet arms of the chair.

"Well," she said, clearing her throat politely. "It's so nice to have you here again."

She paused. The next subject was delicate.

"Do you remember when you were a little girl and came to visit with your mother, how we used to make dresses for you? I thought it might be fun to sew something while you're here. Everyone's at school all day, we'll have lots of spare time."

Anything would look better than the dreary brown sweater and slacks Wilma was wearing. Or the stiff shiny dress she had worn at dinner the night before. What sort of material was it made of? Mrs. Bridgeport had never seen anything like it in the shops she went to.

"After lunch we can go across the street and pick out some material. Carter's has a marvelous yard-goods department. What would you like? A blouse? A dress? Oh, we can make both." Mrs. Bridgeport tried to sound as though she had just this moment thought of sewing *two* things. She intended to make as many as she could, but she couldn't come right

26

out and say, "You need a whole new ward-robe."

The waitresses moved past, skillfully bearing laden trays of food — for other tables. Mrs. Bridgeport wished their order would come so she could eat and not have to think of something to say for a few minutes. She had been trying to think of things to say to Wilma all morning. And now her suggestion to sew hung heavily between them, with nothing to distract their attention from it. Mrs. Bridgeport could only hope Wilma was not offended by the offer. It was one thing to take a little girl of eight or nine and say, "Let's make you a new dress!" and quite another thing to hint to a sensitive teenager that her clothes weren't right.

"I haven't been sewing much lately," Mrs. Bridgeport heard herself chattering on. "I've missed it. I was president of my women's club this year and it kept me busy. But we changed officers in January, so I don't have as much to do now. I'm co-chairman of our Charity Fashion Show, but that's not until June, so I have some spare time now. I'll enjoy sewing again."

Oh, why did I mention the fashion show? Mrs. Bridgeport accused herself. Wilma was a world removed from such events. *"And next we have Madeleine Bridgeport wearing her green chiffon spring gown."* Heads would *turn. There would be a subdued murmur of approval, a genteel sound of gloved hands clapping.*

"Yes, I'll really enjoy sewing again," Mrs. Bridgeport repeated helplessly.

Wilma looked like an owl, blinking behind her heavy glasses.

And yet somehow she also made Mrs. Bridgeport think of a lumbering snail, enclosed and silent, leaving a moist trail across a dark wood floor in some room where Mrs. Bridgeport had never been.

They looked at pattern books, turning the glossy big pages of Vogue and Butterick. They bought soft red material for a dress, blue jersey for a blouse. They left, carrying the rustling parcels, promises of beauty to come for Wilma. But it had been a long day, and Mrs. Bridgeport was glad when it was over.

Her heart lightened as she went to tuck Emily into bed that night. It was an evening ritual she always looked forward to, for it included a kiss on each tiny cheek. Then Emily would close her eyes and Mrs. Bridgeport would kiss each fragile lid.

Charles thought he was too big for goodnight kisses, and Joan's good-night was usually delivered in an offhand manner as she sat propped up in bed writing the events of her day in her diary and listening to music. "Records will be off in a minute," she'd promise.

Only Emily always waited expectantly for a good-night kiss.

But on this particular night Emily looked rather forlorn, and she snuggled the white cat against her face.

"Kitty didn't mean to do anything bad."

"I know, dear. It was just an accident."

Mrs. Bridgeport sat on the edge of the bed and stroked the cat's furry head. "Don't worry anymore about it," she said. "Anna found some pots. I'm sure the plants will be fine."

"Is Anna mad at Kitty?"

"No, of course not. Anna loves Kitty too."

Mrs. Bridgeport lifted the cat and placed it at the foot of Emily's bed. "Go to sleep, Kitty," she said gently. "And you too, *my* little kitty." She edged the covers up around Emily's shoulders.

How small and vulnerable the troubled face looked upon the pillow. Mrs. Bridgeport felt a pang of sadness. Little children were so innocent and trusting.

"Close your eyes." With the tip of a polished nail Mrs. Bridgeport lovingly drew each eye closed.

But the lids opened again, and Emily's brown eyes stared up.

"Mama — can I have my light on?"

Mrs. Bridgeport looked into the dark eyes.

"Your light on?" she repeated blankly. It had been years since Emily had wanted a night-light.

"Can I, Mama?"

"But — why?"

"I want it. I don't like the dark."

"Emily . . ." Mrs. Bridgeport chided with a smile.

"Please, Mama. Can I?"

"But Emily . . ." Mrs. Bridgeport grew more serious. "There's nothing to be afraid of."

It had been so long ago, Mrs. Bridgeport had almost forgotten that, when Emily was two or three, a line of light always showed under her bedroom door at night. And then, when Emily was about five, she didn't need the light at night anymore.

Maybe she was just unhappy because of Anna's plants. It would pass. Mrs. Bridgeport decided to make no issue of the matter.

When she left the room, Emily lay in the glow of lamplight from her bedside table.

And the little white cat had already curled into a ball and gone to sleep.

Mrs. Bridgeport closed the door quietly and went down the hall to her room.

Joan and Wilma were watching the television set in Joan's room as they got ready for bed, but the sound was muted by the closed door. The house seemed completely quiet.

A single lamp was lit in Mrs. Bridgeport's room, and she stood at her dressing table reflectively drawing off her earrings. She unclasped her watch . . . and then, in the mirror, she noticed that something lay on her bed. She turned and studied the square of white. Only when she went closer did she realize what it was: Charles's science notebook.

He had already shown it to her. Had he left it here for her to see again? She lifted the folder, but the front cover, which had so clearly said *Charles Bridgeport — Room 204 — STARS AND PLANETS,* was now obscured by what seemed to be a large waxy blot that covered most of the page. Mrs. Bridgeport scratched at it with a fingernail, leaving thin streaks in the wax.

Why, how could this have happened?

And what a pity, she thought. Charles had worked especially hard on the cover drawing. He had been so proud. . . . She rubbed at the blot, but it would not rub away. Gone from sight behind it were the rings of Saturn and the moons of Jupiter.

Mrs. Bridgeport opened the notebook. Each page was the same: ruined to a more or less degree by dark waxy blotches. Only here and there a word or two remained visible. *Pluto is the newest planet....*

Mrs. Bridgeport felt vexed and sad and suddenly weary. Something had gotten on the cover and seeped all the way through. Charles must be more careful where he laid his things.

Emily's night-light continued to burn as the weekend passed. Each night Mrs. Bridgeport hoped might be the last. Once, waking in the middle of the night, she opened her door and looked down the dark hallway.

Still there, at the bottom of Emily's door, was the line of light.

It gave Mrs. Bridgeport an undefined sense of sorrow. Behind that door a little girl was sleeping. *Her* little girl. With a defenseless white cat curled at her feet.

Mrs. Bridgeport returned to bed and lay awake restlessly. She turned first this way and that, but could not get back to sleep. After what seemed an endless time, she heard the creak of a floorboard in the hall. Was someone up? She strained her ears in the silence. Just when she had convinced herself there was no one in the hall, there was another furtive step, another pause.

Mrs. Bridgeport stared into the darkness, her own heartbeat louder than the sound of the footsteps. Was there a burglar in the house? Trembling, she rose at last and felt for the robe on the chair beside her bed. Moving as quietly as she could, she drew open the bed-table drawer and groped in the dark for the flashlight she kept there.

She opened her door an inch or so and pressed her ear to the opening.

No further sound came from the hall.

And then, in a stillness so thick around her Mrs. Bridgeport felt suffocated by it, she heard another sound begin. But it was not the sound of footsteps. It was the sound of a clock.

Faintly, steadily, in the hushed darkness beyond her room, a clock was ticking.

Mrs. Bridgeport stared down the hall, a prickly feeling along her arms, her heart beating rapidly.

The sound came from the direction of the stairs . . . where the grandfather clock that did not work stood on the landing.

Mrs. Bridgeport eased her door farther open and flashed a beam of light into the hallway. There was no one there. She had been right, of course; the footsteps were only her imagination.

But the clock?

Mrs. Bridgeport paused and listened again. As suddenly as it had begun, the ticking stopped.

Now there was nothing.

Not a sound in all the house.

Mrs. Bridgeport held up her robe with one hand and started down the stairs with the flashlight. When she had gone as far as the landing, she aimed the beam of light upon the clock. It stood as always, the pendulum hanging motionless behind the glimmering reflections that wavered upon the glass door.

Mrs. Bridgeport moved the light upward, to the clock face. The hands stood at twenty minutes to eleven, but she realized with a sense of annoyance that this meant nothing. It had been so long since the clock had run that she had forgotten where the hands had been. They may well have been pointing to twenty minutes to eleven all these months. The clock had been repaired the autumn before: it had kept time for a few weeks, then stopped again. It had been repaired a second time, and stopped again. It had been exasperating.

Surely the ticking must have been her imagination, like the sound of steps in the hall.

The only sound she was sure she had not imagined was the sound of Charles coughing.

She heard this quite distinctly as she passed his door on her way back to bed.

Perhaps he should stay home from school a few days. The damp March weather with its chills and high winds could not be good for him.

But on Monday morning Charles seemed better.

"I think you can go to school," Mrs. Bridgeport said, drawing him close to her chair at the breakfast table and searching his face. A wave of dark hair fell across his forehead. He was such a handsome boy.

"How do you feel?"

"I feel okay."

Emily had her coat on and hopped about from foot to foot, waiting for Charles. Joan had already left for an early class, and Wilma had not yet come downstairs.

A pale sun was shining, its beams lying in thin white patches across the blue carpet. Even this wan sunlight revived Mrs. Bridgeport's spirits after the cloudy weekend, and she patted Charles's shoulder.

"Scoot, then."

When the children had gone she sat at the table, lingering over her coffee and the morning newspaper. Wilma was sleeping late for the first time since she had come, and Mrs.

Bridgeport enjoyed the privacy of the breakfast table, the sense of peace and quiet and the order she always felt when the last coat button had been buttoned, the last scurry for books and mittens was over.

It was just past nine when the phone rang, and Mrs. Arling's voice came over the line. She was co-chairman with Mrs. Bridgeport for the Charity Fashion Show.

"Madeleine," she began in her usual cheery, efficient way, "I was wondering if you could stop by this morning and look at the fashion-show programs I've made up for the printer. The sooner we get them out, the better."

"Yes, of course."

"You're an angel." Mrs. Arling sounded pleased.

Mrs. Bridgeport had begun Wilma's dress over the weekend, and she had planned to continue today. But there would be time enough when she came home. Besides, Wilma was still sleeping.

Wilma came down at ten thirty, just as Mrs. Bridgeport was ready to leave. She stood at the foot of the stairs, her coat on, her dark hair tied back with a green silk scarf.

"This won't take long, Wilma," she explained apologetically. "Anna will fix you some breakfast. This afternoon we can work on the dress."

"That's okay."

Mrs. Bridgeport drew on her gloves. Was there anything else she could say before she left?

"Maybe you can write to your mother this morning," she suggested, to fill the silence, "or some of your friends back home."

Did Wilma have any friends back home to write to? Mrs. Bridgeport pushed things aside in her purse, looking for the car keys.

"I'm sure your mother would enjoy a note."

But if Wilma wrote to her mother or friends, Mrs. Bridgeport never saw the letters. Perhaps Wilma wrote the letters and walked out to mail them while she was gone. Mrs. Bridgeport didn't ask.

The week passed slowly. Wilma spent most of her time lying on Joan's bed watching television. Mrs. Bridgeport could see her when she passed the half-open door. How Wilma could enjoy doing it, Mrs. Bridgeport could not imagine. There was so little that was interesting to watch on daytime television. The thought of someone endlessly watching game shows and soap operas was somehow appalling.

"*And now, what do we have for this lucky couple? . . . What is behind Aladdin's curtain of wonders? . . . A dishwasher? . . . An automobile? . . . A bag of gumdrops? . . . What*

37

will it be? . . . Aladdin's Lamp continues after this message from our sponsors."

Wilma was no trouble, but somehow her presence there, lying upstairs staring at the television screen, gave Mrs. Bridgeport an unsettled feeling she would have found difficult to put into words.

There were occasional dress fittings, and Wilma stood patiently for those. But what went on in her mind Mrs. Bridgeport did not know.

Mrs. Bridgeport had publicity to write for the fashion show, and she occupied herself with that, trying not to think of the monotonous murmur of television voices drifting down to her from the floor above. Once she put on a Chopin record, but Wilma picked just that time to come downstairs and wander about the living room, disturbing the dreamy atmosphere the record had created.

When Wilma went upstairs again, Mrs. Bridgeport sat at her writing desk and pushed aside the club work with a feeling of disinterest. Usually she loved her club work, and the charity fashion show was the main activity of the year. The money would go to a children's summer camp. But she could not get her mind on the fashion show, and after a moment she opened a desk drawer and took out a box of stationery.

Dear Catherine,

We are enjoying Wilma's visit with us so very much. The children are happy to be getting acquainted with their cousin again . . .

Mrs. Bridgeport's pen hesitated over the paper.

Nothing she had written was really true. Charles and Emily were still shy with Wilma, subdued in the presence of the clumsy, blinking girl who stared at them while they ate and appeared around corners when they least expected her. Joan hadn't said anything in so many words, but Mrs. Bridgeport had a feeling she was beginning to long to have her room to herself again. It was hardly like Joan's room anymore, with Wilma always lying on the bed watching television. Did Joan still write in her diary, with Wilma so close every night?

We're making a dress. Mrs. Bridgeport went on with the letter doggedly. *Just like old times. We also have some material for a blouse. Blue. It's such a becoming color for Wilma.*

If anything was "becoming" for Wilma. . . . Mrs. Bridgeport rubbed her forehead. A sense of futility swept over her. Futility for this letter, for her sewing project, for all the dismal days just past.

Joan is having some of her girl friends in for lunch Saturday, to meet Wilma. We want Wilma to have a good time while she's here.

The words of the letter came slow and labored. Mrs. Bridgeport could hardly think of one sentence to follow another. She wrote in large, sweeping strokes, in order to fill the paper sooner, and she sealed the envelope at last with a sigh of relief.

As she turned from her desk she noticed Anna in the doorway, staring at the portrait above the mantel.

"What is it, Anna?"

Anna's broad face had a puzzled expression. "It looks different."

"Different?" Mrs. Bridgeport looked up at the portrait of her children. Her beautiful children. Nothing looked different to her.

Anna stood stoically in the doorway, arms folded across her chest.

Mrs. Bridgeport frowned. There *was* something about the portrait, but she could not say what. Emily's face perhaps . . . it looked thinner in the pale sunlight that slanted across the canvas. Surely it was only the way the light fell. A painting could not change. Emily was not Dorian Gray.

"It's just the light, Anna."

Anna shrugged and went on past the doorway with her firm, plodding step. There was a cake baking in the kitchen, and she had dinner preparations to begin.

Mrs. Bridgeport continued to sit at her desk, the letter to her sister in her hand. She should get on with her club work now. Or perhaps the sewing. She wanted to have the red dress finished in time for the luncheon Saturday.

But it was too late to start anything. The children would be coming home from school soon. Suddenly Mrs. Bridgeport wanted very much to see them — to see Emily's sweet face, hear Joan's laughter, reassure herself that Charles was not feverish again.

She rested her head against the high chair-back and closed her eyes a moment.

Around her, in the luxurious, polished room of the home she loved so much, each vase, figurine, book, sofa pillow was in its place. And the pale afternoon light that touched the portrait above the mantel cast shadows upon the brass andirons on the hearth below.

7

The Saturday luncheon was not completely successful. Joan had somehow felt it wouldn't be — not even with her mother's best silver and china, not even with Anna's friend Mrs.

Cardalla coming to read the girls' fortunes. The luncheon was for Wilma, and doing things with Wilma just wasn't any fun.

Shortly before noon, Joan gave the dining-room table a final survey. Upon a rose-colored cloth her mother's finest china had been set at six places. Two tall pink candles waited to be lit. Water goblets sparkled. Silver gleamed. Joan smoothed a nonexistent wrinkle in the cloth and wandered across the hall to the living room.

From the window she could see a good way down Windsor Drive, where fashionable homes were set well back from the street behind spacious lawns, now drab and faded looking in the aftermath of winter.

In the summer the street was so beautiful. . . . Joan leaned closer to the window and yearned for the green lawns of summer and the dappled pattern of sunlight through the tall elms, for roses blooming on white trellises, and petunia beds along the driveways.

Even winter was beautiful on Windsor Drive, the bushes white with snow, Christmas-tree lights in the windows.

But March was so dreary, *neither winter nor spring*.

And how especially dreary the last week had been, since Wilma came.

Joan had remembered her cousin as a plump,

dowdy girl, and even when she saw that Wilma hadn't changed she wasn't discouraged. She had cherished her "Cinderella" plan. With Joan to help her, applying just the right shade of lipstick, arranging a new hairstyle, Wilma would soon be transformed into a true beauty. A diet and the right clothes would make her look thinner. How surprised everybody would be.

But none of this had come about.

Joan had realized almost at once that it had been a crazy idea. Wilma's hair was too limp and colorless; no new hairstyle would help. And there never seemed a diplomatic time to suggest a new lipstick. Not even the new red dress helped much.

There was nothing that could be done for Wilma.

The luncheon, which at first had seemed a good idea to Joan, now appeared as ill conceived as her "Cinderella" plan, and Joan wished it were over. Wilma would sit and stare and not say anything. She would look more awkward and dull than ever in the midst of Joan's pretty girl friends.

If I were poor and homely, Joan thought as she gazed out of the window, I wouldn't want to sit around with pretty girls in pretty clothes — girls who were at ease together, giggling, chattering, flashing dazzling smiles, and tossing long, shiny hair.

No cars came circling into the drive beside the house, and Joan sighed again as she watched and waited. Her thoughts shifted from Wilma to her girl friends. Cissy Allen ... Gina ... what would they think of Wilma? It began to seem harder and harder to face the introductions and the luncheon, which had already grown to interminable proportions in Joan's mind. She wished her mother would get back from whatever errand had taken her out on this particular morning and at this least-convenient time. If Wilma sat and stared and didn't say anything, Mother would know what to do to make everybody feel at ease.

Suddenly Joan felt a presence in the room with her and she turned from the window hopefully.

"Mother . . .?" But there was no one there.

The room was empty. Everything was in order, ready for the guests. The flame flickered in the fireplace. There was candy in silver dishes on the tables. But the room was empty.

From the kitchen beyond the dining room Joan could hear muted sounds of activity as Anna finished the luncheon preparations. Emily and Charles would be watching, sampling olives and picking crumbs from the cake pans. Joan wondered for a moment if one of them had come to peek and see if the company was here.

But as she looked across the hall and up the stairway, she was somehow certain that it had been Wilma who had come and stood by the living-room door, and then run away. Wilma was always sort of slinking around, appearing unexpectedly in doorways and around the turn of the stairs. Joan didn't like the feeling that while she had stood at the window Wilma had been behind her, spying. It wasn't a nice feeling.

Joan went up the stairs cautiously and pushed open the bedroom door. Wilma sat at the dressing table brushing her dingy hair. The belt to the red dress lay across the bed.

"Ready yet?" Joan tried to sound nonchalant.

"I guess so," Wilma answered without expression. Her face looked bleak and exposed without her glasses.

Do something, Joan wanted to shout, and as though she had read Joan's thoughts, Wilma put down the hairbrush and put on her glasses.

Now she was the same old Wilma.

She fastened her belt without looking in the mirror, and it was slightly off-center. Then she just stood there, as dowdy and dull looking as ever. It was as though she were deliberately trying to look as bad as she could, Joan thought, as though she were saying, "See, this dress doesn't help at all."

Joan wanted to say, "Straighten your belt. Smile. Don't just stand there."

But she didn't say anything. She didn't care if Wilma's belt was crooked. She didn't care whether Wilma smiled or not. Even the pretty new dress couldn't make Wilma pretty. And Joan didn't care. She just wished Wilma would go home.

"Let's go down then, if you're ready."

"Might as well." Wilma pushed at her glasses with a nail-bitten finger.

"Oh! Someone's here." The bell had rung in the hall below, and Joan darted to the stairs and ran down ahead of Wilma.

Wilma came along slowly, chewing her lip. She could hear the sound of voices in the hall, the commotion and chatter of high-school girls, sounds Wilma remembered very well from her abandoned school days — the laughter and talking-together from which she had always been cut off, an outsider.

At school she had been able to get away. She just kept walking right past the girls who clustered at an open locker, at a lunchroom table, at a classroom desk. She just kept her eyes down and walked past.

But she couldn't do that now.

She would have to go on down into the hall.

She would be surrounded. She would be stared at. She would be whispered about behind the water goblets and the burning candles.

Her hands were clammy, and she rubbed them against the skirt of her new dress. However slowly she dragged along, the stairs went by one by one. She turned on the landing, and now she could see the girls in the hall, taking off their coats, running fingers through silky hair. All their clothes were bright and beautiful. Bracelets jangled with a gay party sound.

"Here's Wilma!" Joan was looking toward the stairs, and the other girls turned to look too.

Wilma's mouth was dry. She wished she were a million miles away.

"Come on, slowpoke!" Joan teased. She had her arm looped through another girl's. She was drawing everybody with her to the foot of the stairs.

"Come on and meet Wilma."

Mrs. Bridgeport had been purposefully vague about her errand that Saturday morning. It was not something she wanted to talk about, not even to Joan, whom she often took into her confidence.

She sat restlessly in Dr. Devon's waiting room, rehearsing what she would say. She could not place exactly when she had begun having difficulty sleeping. Had it been before Wilma came? Dates blurred in her mind.

The night she thought she heard footsteps and then heard the clock ticking? Had that been the first night?

No. There had been nights before, nights when she had lain awake regretting her invitation to Wilma and struggling with self-recriminations that she was so unhospitable, so unsympathetic as to feel this regret. A visit of a few weeks was such a simple thing, the least she could do. Yet she was sorry about the whole affair.

One night she had thought she heard laughter in the hall. A low, secretive laughter. No one was there, of course. It had all been her imagination, like the footsteps and the ticking clock.

Yet the fact remained: imagination or not, she could not sleep. She felt tired and irritable and on edge. Little tasks seemed large, the childrens' voices too loud, the harsh March winds unsettling, and the bleak days depressing. What she wanted was a prescription for a mild sedative, without having to explain too much, without having any lecture from Dr. Devon about the risk of depending on sleeping tablets.

She flipped the pages of a magazine, indifferent to the latest fashions, which would normally have entranced her. Her thoughts wandered to the house on Windsor Drive as the clock on the waiting-room wall crept on toward noon. She should be home: But Anna could handle everything, and Mrs. Bridgeport felt wanly content to be where she was. Here in the impersonal, hushed-voice atmosphere of the waiting room she was free of the responsibilities of home.

"Dr. Devon will see you now, Mrs. Bridgeport."

The nurse's voice was the calm, detached voice of every nurse in every doctor's waiting room. Nurses had no troubles, Mrs. Bridgeport thought. Other people had troubles. Other people came to see doctors. But the nurses, receptionists, assistants — they were forever safely beyond whatever strains and pains afflicted the rest of the world. They rustled patient's record files, wore starchy white uniforms and soft-soled shoes, said, "The doctor will see you now."

"Thank you." Mrs. Bridgeport put aside the magazine she had not really been reading and smoothed her skirt as she stood up.

And of course, her thoughts moved on, she should tell Dr. Devon about Charles, about how lately he always seemed on the verge of a cold or fever, flushed and pale by turns, never quite well.

She was not long in the doctor's office, and the girls had not even reached dessert when she returned to Windsor Drive. She chatted with them briefly. . . .

Cissy Allen was as lively as ever, although she gushed a little too much for Mrs. Bridgeport's taste. "Oh, Mrs. Bridgeport, everything is so *good*. And your plates are *beautiful*!" Cissy's blue eyes sparkled. "I wish my mother would get some just like them."

"Thank you, Cissy."

"This chicken salad is the best I ever tasted!"

Mrs. Bridgeport's attention drifted to Wilma in her new red dress. The girl looked rather lost, and Mrs. Bridgeport smiled encouragingly. As the afternoon went on, Wilma would get to know the other girls better, and maybe she would talk more. Anyway, Mrs. Cardalla was coming at one o'clock to read palms, and that would keep everybody busy.

Mrs. Cardalla did come at one o'clock, but she read no palms.

Mrs. Bridgeport was in the kitchen with Anna when Mrs. Cardalla rapped at the back door. But when Anna opened the door, Mrs. Cardalla did not step in.

Mrs. Bridgeport could feel the cold air, and she wondered why Anna and her friend stood talking in the open doorway. She couldn't hear what they were saying, except a word now and then.

"No." Mrs. Cardalla's face was inscrutable. She seemed more shrunken and wrinkled than Mrs. Bridgeport remembered as she stood there in a shapeless coat, her head swathed in a coarsely knit shawl. She looked as though she had just arrived from the old country. A true gypsy.

Anna had met her a few months before at — of all places! — a séance. Since then reports of Mrs. Cardalla's amazing powers had fascinated the Bridgeport children. Mrs. Cardalla could talk to spirits from the other world; she could read palms, tarot cards, tea leaves, and something she called "vibrations."

Mrs. Bridgeport herself had been more amused than impressed at these tales of Mrs. Cardalla, with whom Anna had quickly fallen into the habit of sharing her afternoons off. But Mrs. Bridgeport saw no harm in the woman, or in Anna's devotion to her. It interfered in no way with Anna's duties as housekeeper — although Mrs. Bridgeport would have been rather surprised to see the books of occult mystery Mrs. Cardalla gave Anna to read.

The cold air continued to come into the kitchen from the open door. And then, instead of Mrs. Cardalla's coming in, Anna went out to the back steps.

"The girls are waiting," Mrs. Bridgeport said. She frowned. Whatever was the matter with Mrs. Cardalla? Why didn't she come in?

Mrs. Bridgeport could not hear any further words as Mrs. Cardalla's voice sank to an undertone — and yet she continued to speak in a rapid stream as she stood with one hand upon Anna's arm. Her great eyes rolled in her head.

"Anna, the door," Mrs. Bridgeport reminded the housekeper politely. She was getting chilled. "Won't you come in, Mrs. Cardalla . . .?" But her voice faded away as, to her surprise, Mrs. Cardalla turned abruptly and hurried off. Anna hesitated a moment and then came back into the kitchen with a downcast expression.

Mrs. Bridgeport could see Mrs. Cardalla's shawled head retreating to the back gate.

"What on earth . . .?" Mrs. Bridgeport was baffled.

"She will not come in," Anna said.

"Not come in? But she's supposed to tell fortunes."

Anna shook her head. "There is something wrong here. Mrs. Cardalla will not come in."

Mrs. Bridgeport felt the frustration and

irritation of the past week pour over her. This was the last straw.

"What nonsense, Anna."

"There *is* something wrong," Anna repeated doggedly.

Mrs. Bridgeport felt at a loss for words. Something wrong! The whole week had been gloomy and dismal. Everyone was tired of hearing the wind, tired of misty, dark days. It was March. A dreadful month.

But whatever had got into Mrs. Cardalla's head, she was gone now. There would be no fortune-telling, and the girls had been looking forward to it.

Mrs. Bridgeport unexplainably felt close to tears. There was nothing to cry about, she told herself. She was just overtired. Now she had some pills from Dr. Devon, and tonight she would sleep. But her mouth trembled, and her eyes followed Anna anxiously. The lunch dishes were in the dishwasher; the kitchen was tidy for Mrs. Cardalla's arrival. Anna had been heating water to make Mrs. Cardalla a cup of tea. Now she turned the burner off under the kettle and went to her room. She closed the door and left Mrs. Bridgeport standing alone in the kitchen.

8

On the following Tuesday afternoon. Dr. Devon stopped by at Windsor Drive. He was an old family friend as well as family doctor, and Mrs. Bridgeport greeted him with delight.

"James, what a pleasant surprise."

Dr. Devon was a portly gentleman with a high-domed forehead and kindly blue eyes. He held Mrs. Bridgeport at arm's length for a moment and nodded approvingly.

"You're looking better, Madeleine."

"I'm feeling much better, now that I've had a few nights' rest."

He lifted a finger playfully and chided, "Mustn't get too dependent on those sleeping pills."

"You know I won't. Do you have time for coffee?" She led him into the living room, and he settled into a comfortable chair by the fire while she spoke to Anna.

It was one of those dreary March afternoons when the chill and grayness of the weather outside made the indoors glow with light and warmth and coziness by contrast. It was a time of year for *rooms*. For golden rings of lamplight on tabletops, the flicker of firelight behind a grate, a friend visiting, muted sounds of coffee cups on a tray, the glint of silver as a cream pitcher was lifted.

The doctor sat back with a relaxed and unhurried manner and gazed appreciatively around the room before turning to smile at Mrs. Bridgeport.

"Yes, you do look better. And how is Charles?"

Mrs. Bridgeport felt apologetic. Dr. Devon had given her a prescription for Charles, and she wanted to tell him that it had been a wonderful success. But that wouldn't have been true.

"I'm afraid he doesn't seem much better. He's taken the medicine you prescribed, but ..." She concluded the sentence with a regretful expression.

"Umm." Dr. Devon tugged at his lower lip, considering what she had said.

"In fact, I kept him home from school today."

"Well, then," the doctor said, "perhaps I'd better have a look at him."

"I wish you would."

Mrs. Bridgeport went upstairs at once to bring Charles from his room. As she passed the door to Joan's room she could see Wilma sitting by the window, her arms on the sill, her head bent forward. The television set was on, but Wilma's back was to it. What went on in her mind? Mrs. Bridgeport wondered, as she had wondered a hundred times. Wilma had probably seen Dr. Devon's car, but if she heard Mrs. Bridgeport in the hall she did not turn to ask who had come.

Charles's door was closed, and Mrs. Bridgeport opened it to find Charles sitting at his desk and putting together one of the model cars he liked to tinker with. He was wearing pajamas and a robe, from which the untied belt drooped loosely, spreading its tasseled end on the floor by the chair.

"Darling, Dr. Devon's here. Come down a minute and let him have a look at you."

"I'm all right," Charles protested. He turned a peaked face and listless eyes in her direction. "I could have gone to school."

"He just wants to see you a minute. You can get right back to your car."

Charles followed his mother reluctantly, his belt trailing. It was easier to sit upstairs. He didn't really feel like walking much.

Mrs. Bridgeport sat in a wing chair as Dr. Devon examined Charles. Her coffee had grown cold on the tray.

"When Dr. Devon's through, you can have some cookies," she said.

But Charles shook his head without interest. "They hurt my throat."

"That medicine should help your throat," Dr. Devon said. He had gotten his bag from the car and drew out a thermometer. "Have you been taking it every day?"

Charles nodded, and Mrs. Bridgeport said, "Yes, of course, three times a day, just as you prescribed."

"It should have helped by now. Well, let's see." Dr. Devon put the thermometer in Charles's mouth. "How are the other children? Any signs of colds or sore throats?"

"They're fine," Mrs. Bridgeport said. "It's only Charles."

After a moment or two Dr. Devon examined the thermometer. "He has a slight temperature. But nothing much, really. Let's see that throat now, young man."

"Maybe he needs vitamins or something," Mrs. Bridgeport suggested.

"Couldn't do any harm." Dr. Devon smiled. "Your throat looks fine, Charles. Sure those cookies would be too much for you?"

"They hurt my throat," Charles insisted.

"Maybe you should get in bed, darling, instead of working on that car."

"But I *want* to," Charles begged. His dark hair was tangled moistly on his forehead. "I don't want to go to bed."

"He's making a model car." Mrs. Bridgeport looked at Dr. Devon for his opinion.

"I don't think that would do any harm, for a little while," Dr. Devon said, and Charles went back upstairs with his trailing belt.

"Hard to keep youngsters in bed." The doctor's coffee had grown cold too, but he lifted the cup and drank it graciously. "Still, rest is important." His manner grew more serious. "Are you sure Charles gets enough rest? He's not working too hard at school?"

"I don't think so." Mrs. Bridgeport had a sense of disorientation. How long had it been since Charles had come bursting in with some school news? How long had it been since she had even asked him about school . . . or felt any interest in her committee work . . . or bothered to check the dinner menus with Anna . . . ? Somehow the past days she had felt a separation from reality. First she had thought it was because she couldn't sleep at night. Lack of sleep throws everything out of proportion. Now that she had the sleeping pills, she thought it must be the pills that left her with a detached feeling.

. . . Or was she, subconsciously, waiting for Wilma to go and for life to fall back into its familiar pattern? There had been no letters or phone calls from Catherine saying "We miss Wilma, send her home." How long was Wilma going to stay? Mrs. Bridgeport longed for the peace and privacy of her own home, her own family again. It would be easier to think about other things then. She would get back to her committee work. Everything would be all right.

"Is anything wrong, Madeleine?"

She became aware that Dr. Devon was looking at her curiously. He had asked about Charles and school. . . . She struggled to bring her thoughts back.

"No, I don't think he's working too hard at school. He likes school, and he always does well. It's not really work for him. He learns everything so quickly, so easily. He's a natural student."

Dr. Devon was regarding her thoughtfully, and Mrs. Bridgeport knew she was rattling on, but she couldn't stop. "My niece has been visiting us the last couple of weeks. I was wondering, do you suppose Charles could be, well, upset in some way? There is a certain balance to a household, and I've heard that upsetting that balance sometimes affects children. Emily asked for a night-light after Wilma came, and she hasn't needed one for *years*. Do you suppose the whole thing has somehow affected Charles in just this particular way of not feeling well?"

The idea sounded farfetched, and Mrs.

Bridgeport felt embarrassed. But Dr. Devon was understanding and kind, and she was grateful now that he did not laugh at her or scold her for such a foolish idea. He was always calm and reassuring.

"I would guess it's all just coincidence, Madeleine. How old is Emily now? Seven, eight? Little children sometimes do revert to baby habits. Let her have the light and don't make any fuss."

"I haven't." Mrs. Bridgeport clutched her fingers together. She was surprised to find they trembled, and she clenched them, hoping Dr. Devon would not notice.

"As for Charles, when he's had another day or so of that medicine, you'll see a change. I'll warrant that he *has* been overdoing somewhere along the line — at school or whatever — and you didn't realize it. He's more rundown than anything. Intelligent children are often high-strung. Perhaps he puts more intensity into his schoolwork than you realize."

"Yes, perhaps he does." Mrs. Bridgeport smiled gratefully.

Anna brought fresh coffee. The lamplight glowed, casting images upon the windows where the cold of afternoon crept up but could not get in.

"Shall we have a glass of sherry with our coffee?" Mrs. Bridgeport suggested. She really was beginning to feel better about things. Everything was so logical and reasonable and in order when Dr. Devon was there.

But at last it was time for him to go. Mrs. Bridgeport knew, just by the way he set his glass on the table and straightened his shoulders, that he was going to leave. The firelight, the lamplight, the golden sherry in long-stemmed glasses would not be the same when he had gone. The house would be quiet again, with Wilma watching television and Charles sick in his room.

Mrs. Bridgeport wanted to keep Dr. Devon in the house, and knew she couldn't, or shouldn't. He had already lingered longer than she expected.

"I've got to get back on the job," Dr. Devon declared, even while Mrs. Bridgeport was having these thoughts. "Can't keep everybody waiting."

"Who's waiting?" She tried to sound light and cheerful. Inside, a dull heaviness was settling into her body.

"Women having babies, for one." Dr. Devon was buttoning his coat. "Gallbladders, appendixes, you name it. And — " he glanced at a handsome gold wristwatch — "an angry nurse, I'm afraid. It's after three, and I told her I'd be in by two thirty."

Mrs. Bridgeport could picture the waiting

room. There was a rubber plant by the window. A *Vogue* magazine she had not read. And the nurse in her white dress. *The doctor will see you now.*

Mrs. Bridgeport felt bereft to see Dr. Devon walking along the driveway toward his car. She had a sense of abandonment that she could not rationalize.

Long after he could possibly see her, she stood by the door waving.

Then she stepped back into the house and closed the door.

His presence had been comforting — he was such a good, stable, considerate man. But now she was alone again.

Mrs. Bridgeport stood by the closed door, feeling the knob cold against her hand. She looked ahead into the house: the green entrance hall, the living-room doorway to the left, the stairway to the right.

She had felt . . . well, *protected* was the word . . . protected while Dr. Devon had been sitting by the fireplace drinking coffee and sipping sherry. And now he was gone, sure in his mind that everything was all right — that Charles only needed rest and medicine, that it was not unusual for Emily to ask for a nightlight, that Mrs. Bridgeport would not take too many sleeping tablets; feeling that there was nothing wrong in the Bridgeport house.

And yet Mrs. Bridgeport thought of scenes from movies and TV shows — scenes where a person in trouble, held captive, tries to write a secret SOS note . . . but a hand comes onto the screen and crumples the note before it is finished. She thought of scenes where casual friends call under the assumption that everything is all right. There were victims, guns at their backs and a voice saying, "Answer the door, talk natural." The victims did. They answered the door and talked natural. No one suspected danger. The caller left, thinking all was well.

Mrs. Bridgeport felt now as though she had tried to send an SOS, tried to call for help in some way obscure even to herself. But the helper was gone. She had been left alone in a house where Dr. Devon thought everything was all right.

9

That night Mrs. Bridgeport made up her mind not to take a sedative. Three nights in a row was enough. She had promised Dr. Devon she would not become dependent on them. And perhaps it was not really good to be sleeping so soundly all through the night. What if something happened? What if there was some trouble in the night and she didn't wake up?

After the children had gone to bed, Mrs. Bridgeport deliberately stayed up late to make herself sleepy. She sat on the apricot-colored sofa by the fireplace and read until her eyelids felt heavy. But even so, when she went to bed at last, she could not fall asleep. She switched on the bedside lamp and looked at the small gold clock on the table. Two thirty. She looked again at three fifteen. At four o'clock she got up and stood aimlessly by the window. A pale moon had risen, and an eerie light spread across the rooftops and gardens along Windsor Drive. There was not a car in sight, and the streetlamps stood like silent sentinels. The scene had the quality of a ghostly landscape, and Mrs. Bridgeport turned away with a gesture of distress. All the world was asleep but her.

Without any real purpose, she went to her door and stood listening. Was it too late to take a sleeping pill now? Perhaps she should give up sleeping altogether and read awhile. But her book was downstairs in the living room, and she felt an unexplainable hesitancy to go through the dark, deserted house — the house she loved so much it was like part of her very blood and bones. She had supervised every bit of decorating, chosen each piece of furniture, each lamp and vase and carpet. But now she did not want to leave her room.

As she stood by the door, she could hear the clock ticking on the landing below; perhaps she had really come to the door to listen for it, to assure herself it wasn't ticking and never had been. And now she heard it. Tick-tock, tick-tock, tick-tock, calling her to come-see, come-see, come-see.

Mrs. Bridgeport once again took the flashlight from its place and opened her door.

But now the ticking had stopped.

The hall was completely silent.

And yet, as she gazed into the darkness, something nagged at her mind. Something had changed. Not just the clock stopping. Something else had changed.

And then she realized what it was. There was no light under Emily's door. It had been there when Mrs. Bridgeport came to bed at one o'clock, and it was certainly unlikely that Emily had awakened since then and turned her night-light off. That missing line of light gave Mrs. Bridgeport an uneasy feeling, as though something secret had happened while she lay trying to sleep. Things should not change at night when everyone is in bed.

Things should be the same in the morning. Lights left on at night should still be burning when morning came, even though they burned then in sunny rooms.

It was probably only that the bulb had gone out . . . but Emily would be frightened if she awoke before morning and found herself in the dark.

Surely it was only that, a burned-out bulb. But even so, Mrs. Bridgeport could not shake her sense of uneasiness as she went along the hall and opened the door to Emily's room. She moved the flashlight cautiously. Emily slept on soundly, and the white cat curled up at the foot of the bed did not stir.

Mrs. Bridgeport tiptoed to the bedside table and touched the lamp switch. Light blazed. There was nothing wrong with the bulb at all. Mrs. Bridgeport tried the switch a time or two, and it was working perfectly. She frowned to herself. Now that was strange. How had the light gone off? She glanced around the room, aiming the flashlight beam into dark corners, looking for she knew not what . . . looking to see that everything was really all right in Emily's room.

On the wall by Emily's bureau there seemed to be some marks, and Mrs. Bridgeport moved closer. Now what was *this*? But as she came closer the marks faded away. She paused, staring, and then touched her fingers to the wall, but there was nothing there. She rubbed her eyes, strained from reading so long downstairs. What tricks they played in the wavering light.

Mrs. Bridgeport moved slowly toward the door. Emily stretched and turned her head, but did not waken, and Mrs. Bridgeport left her sleeping safely in the lamplight.

When she was in the hall again, Mrs. Bridgeport remembered the clock. She stood a moment, listening. But no sound came from the landing. If the ticking had been her imagination again, there was now a sure way to find out. She knew where the hands of the clock had been that other night — which seemed so long ago. She would go and look and find them pointing still to twenty minutes to eleven. Then she would know she had only *thought* she heard ticking. Then she could go back to bed in peace. Then she could sleep.

Through the silence, past the closed doors of the children's rooms, Mrs. Bridgeport went down to the landing and flashed her light upon the clock face.

The hands stood at fifteen minutes past eleven.

She stared in disbelief, her mind rushing from thought to thought. Was she really sure the hands had been at twenty minutes to eleven? Had she gotten the time wrong in her mind somehow? Mrs. Bridgeport forced herself to remember, to remember *correctly*. And by and by she couldn't remember at all. She was not sure *what* time the clock had said before. The more she tried to grasp and pull back the memory, the farther it fled from her.

The first dusky light of morning was beginning to come. There was no point in trying to sleep now. Soon it would be daylight, and all the mysterious darkness of night would be gone. Anna would be busy in the kitchen, the children would come running downstairs for breakfast. Everything would be happy and normal, and all her night fears would vanish with the shadows.

She would make herself some coffee and just relax until the children woke up.

Mrs. Bridgeport went on down the stairs and into the kitchen, a room unfamiliar to her at this early before-dawn hour. She moved about as quietly as she could, so as not to disturb Anna in the adjoining room. She made instant coffee, being sure to take the kettle off before it whistled. She set her cup upon the saucer so that it did not make a sound, carried the coffee into the living room, and pulled open the draperies to watch the morning come.

Mrs. Bridgeport was never up at this time, midway between night and day, and she stood a moment looking at the street. The street-lamps were still lit. What time did they go off? she wondered. There was still no car, no sign of life anywhere beyond the window.

She sat down at last and looked at the portrait of the children, remembering when it had been painted. It had been such a happy time. All of the children had thought it was great fun to pose. And at last, when it was finished, how pleased she had been. She had chosen the luxurious frame, chosen the area above the mantel. Where else did family portraits belong! It had become the focal point of the room, large, impressive, splendid.

But somehow now in the early light, the portrait did not seem quite so beautiful. Mrs. Bridgeport set down her cup and went to stand before the cold fireplace, gazing up at the painting for a long time. The artist had not quite succeeded in capturing Charles's good looks, after all, she thought. Charles was really so much more handsome. He looked pallid, now that Mrs. Bridgeport peered more closely. The hand holding the book was small and limp. She had never noticed it before. And Joan seemed to be shrinking back behind the others. The artist had put her behind Charles and Emily because she was the tallest, but Mrs. Bridgeport thought now that this was wrong, that Joan was too far back.

I'm just tired and irritable and ready to criticize everything, Mrs. Bridgeport thought to herself. She turned away from the portrait with weariness. In the gloom of predawn light nothing looked right or beautiful. Everything was muted and dull and forlorn.

She stood looking about the room with a sense of melancholy. Was this the same room Dr. Devon had chatted in so pleasantly only the afternoon before? It had been such a bright, cozy room then. Now it was gray and lonely, and the street beyond made a desolate picture through the windows. The streetlights burned on as morning came. And a thin circle of moon was still visible as the sky grew light.

It was hours too soon to be up. Tears trembled in Mrs. Bridgeport's eyes. She left the coffee cup where she had set it on a table, went back through the hall and up the stairs, past the silent clock reflecting her shadow on its glass door, past Emily's room, where the line of lamplight showed.

I've been awake all night, Mrs. Bridgeport thought with dismay. I have been awake all night while everyone was sleeping. She felt light-headed with fatigue, and the day ahead was filled with the endless hours and mountainous duties that weigh so hard upon someone who has not slept.

10

The morning sky did not grow very bright, and it began to darken again before noon. By mid-afternoon a misty rain began to fall, as it had the day Wilma arrived.

It's just like that first day I came, Wilma thought.

Emily had come from school with raindrops glistening on her hair. Charles had run in with his wonderful science notebook. Wilma had not had the new red dress then. . . . Even now that she had it, she had only worn it once, at the Saturday lunch. She had wanted to have her fortune told, but the woman had not come.

"Mrs. Cardalla isn't feeling well today," Aunt Madeleine had said.

Wilma remembered this now as she lay on Joan's bed watching television. She wished she could have had her fortune told. What would her fortune be? What would her life be? She had looked for jobs, but nobody wanted to hire her. . . . Maybe they would if she had some pretty clothes.

Aunt Madeleine was going to make the blue blouse next. The pattern was already cut. But

Aunt Madeleine had a headache, and she had gone to lie down in her room instead.

Wilma liked Joan's room when she could be alone there — when Joan was at school. Then she could pretend it was *her* room, that the clothes in the closet were *her* clothes, that the pictures stuck in the mirror frame were pictures of *her* friends.

Wilma's imagination roamed beyond the bedroom. She could pretend the whole house was hers. The whole big, gorgeous house. The maid downstairs was *her* maid.

What would you like for dinner, madam?

Oh, let me think, Anna. Strawberry short- cake would be good.

And if she didn't look in the mirror she could even pretend she was beautiful. She felt beautiful in Joan's room. It was decorated in green and white and lavender. There were bright record album covers and art deco post- ers. Wilma's favorite was a lady sitting on a golden halfmoon. *Vogue* — November 15, 1917.

Oh, yes, Joan Bridgeport had everything anybody could want. A beautiful room. Stereo. Television. Ladies on golden moons.

But even Joan had problems. Last night she had tried to work on a homework paper for school.

"Oh, rats!" she had muttered.

Wilma pretended not to hear.

Joan crumpled the sheet of notebook paper into a ball and fired it at the wastebasket.

But *you* don't have trouble in school, Wilma thought. You don't have trouble, Joan. *I* had trouble in school. . . . "Wilma doesn't understand algebra." . . . "Wilma doesn't know a noun from a verb." . . . *Parlez-vous français?* . . . Not Wilma.

"Do I have to take French?" Wilma stood in Mrs. Webb's office, fat and awkward. The windows were open and a fly came in, buzzing above the cabinets. It was September. Sunlight streamed across the room.

"You have to have a language," Mrs. Webb said. She was always stern. She never smiled. She never understood. She took up a pen and wrote on the card, signing Wilma up for French classes.

Parlez-vous français?

Not Wilma.

Not ever.

But she couldn't forget the office and the sunlight and the lazy fly crawling on the cabinets. She was watching television, but it was Mrs. Webb's face she saw on the screen.

Outside, the misty rain became a thin fog, settling through the streets, giving Windsor Drive the white look of a winter day.

Wilma liked the fog. It reminded her of movies she had seen. There was a subtle excitement about the blurred houses, the haze in the distance. Windsor Drive was only one block long this afternoon.

Anna did *not* like the fog. She trudged back to the bus stop from a visit to Mrs. Cardalla's house. A visit to Mrs. Cardalla meant a bus ride, and damp days made Anna's bones ache. But she had gone anyway.

She knew in her mind that Mrs. Cardalla had been right not to come in to read fortunes. There *was* something wrong in the house. Anna didn't know what it was exactly. Evil spirits, she supposed. She sometimes heard steps behind her when no one was there. She heard sounds at night that she could not explain. But Mrs. Cardalla would know. So she had gone to see Mrs. Cardalla.

They sat in the back parlor of Mrs. Cardalla's little house. Orange peels from Mrs. Cardalla's lunch gave the room a pungent odor. Stuffed birds with glass eyes peered down from a high bookcase. All the furniture was dark and old. The front parlor, reserved for séances, was sealed off behind a sliding door. In that sacred place seven chairs, never more, never less, were set about a round table in the center of the room. Heavy curtains were drawn at the windows. It was always night-time there.

But there was no séance this afternoon.

Only Anna and Mrs. Cardalla were in the back parlor.

Mrs. Cardalla made a pot of the strong spiced tea she liked so well, and sat brooding at her gnarled hands while Anna told her story.

Then she told Anna what to do.

Anna reached the bus stop just as the bus came, glowing with light through the white mist. She boarded and took a seat midway back. Often she had to wait for the bus. It was a barren corner by a vacant lot, with no shelter from wind or rain or snow if the weather was bad. Catching a bus just as she arrived there should have made her feel good — or at least better. Weren't shared troubles lightened by half? But Anna's heart was now heavier than ever, and she sat glumly on the homeward bus, seeing nothing through the misted windows. It was her day off, and only half used up, but she had nowhere else to go.

In the seat ahead a small child rubbed his palm on the window and tried to see through.

"Stop wriggling," the child's mother scolded.

Anna did not want to leave Windsor Drive. Mrs. Cardalla had said she should. But it was not a decision to make in a moment. Everything was so nice there. Anna liked the house best of any she had ever worked in. And suppose Mrs. Cardalla was wrong. Anna gnawed her lip and hoisted herself up as her stop drew near.

What if she left Mrs. Bridgeport and ended up with a woman like Mrs. Lauren, her last employer? Nothing suited Mrs. Lauren. Nothing pleased her. And her children were noisy and spoiled.

Mrs. Bridgeport was pleasant and appreciative of Anna's efforts. She praised Anna's cooking. The children were good. Anna never wanted to shoo them out of the kitchen. Emily stirred cake batter and Charles always had exciting things to tell about school and his playground adventures. He loved riddles and jokes.

"Anna, what has fifty teeth but no mouth?"

He would hold the riddle book behind his back as though she might peek and see the answer from all the way across the kitchen.

"Ach, who knows?" She would pretend not to care.

But he knew she cared. He would stand grinning with glee to have stumped her, and Emily would rush around behind him, practically standing on her head to see the book held upside down behind his back.

"Give up? Give up?" Charles would chant. "It's a comb! A comb, Anna!"

Oh, they were something, those precious children.

Anna lumbered down the bus steps and trudged through the fog toward Windsor Drive. It was a three-block walk, and her legs ached before she got there. A block away she began fumbling in her pocketbook for the key, which always slipped to the bottom and was hard to find.

But she did not need the key after all. As she went up the steps she saw that the back door stood wide open. Chill air swept through the deserted kitchen. Anna tramped through the rooms to find the culprit — but the children were not even home from school yet. There was no one downstairs at all. And every other door and window stood properly closed, though all the lower rooms were drafty. The door had been open a good long time, Anna thought.

She took off her coat and sat at the kitchen table, going over again in her mind all that Mrs. Cardalla had said.

Mrs. Cardalla had said to leave.

Anna considered the whole matter with a trouble face.

At four o'clock Joan rapped at her mother's bedroom door. There was no answer, and after a moment Joan turned the doorknob.

"Mother?"

Mrs. Bridgeport opened dark-shadowed eyes, and Joan came to sit on the edge of the bed.

"Are you sick?"

"Just a headache," Mrs. Bridgeport answered wanly.

Joan hesitated. Her mother was always up, busy with club work or errands, or sometimes having a late-afternoon cup of coffee in the living room as she waited for everyone to come home from school. It was never like *this*.

And she didn't know how to break the news.

"Mother ... Kitty's gone."

"Gone? What do you mean, 'gone'?" Mrs. Bridgeport, only half awake, stared at Joan from the shimmer of satin sheets.

"Just gone." Joan's voice trembled. "I came home from school, and Anna said Emmy and Charles are out looking for her.

Mrs. Bridgeport sat up and pushed at her tousled hair. Joan's face was indistinct in the darkened room, but there was no missing the distress in her voice.

"Out looking for her? But she can't have gotten out. How could she?"

"Anna said the kitchen door was open when she came back today. Kitty could have run out then."

What *else* can go wrong? Mrs. Bridgeport wondered, drugged with sleep. Her head ached.

A dreadful weariness dragged at her body. But she knew she must go downstairs and take charge, comfort Emily.

"Hand me my robe."

"Anna says she knows she didn't leave the door open when she went out."

"Maybe the door wasn't closed tight, and the wind blew it open. Oh, I don't know!" Mrs. Bridgeport could not think clearly. "Open the blind, Joan."

Mrs. Bridgeport's head throbbed. . . . What was she doing in bed in the middle of the day? It would be her fault if anything happened to the dear little white cat.

She felt she could not bear another rainy, gloomy, damp, miserable March day.

If only my head didn't hurt, Mrs. Bridgeport thought, watching numbly as Joan went to the window and lifted her arm to draw open the blind . . . and suddenly she had a queer feeling as she looked at the figure outlined against the window. It could be *anyone* standing there in the room with her. It was Joan, of course, but it could be *anyone*. The dark was deceptive.

"Turn on a light, Joan."

The bedside lamp clicked on, and Joan straightened up, her dark hair swinging.

It was good to see her, Mrs. Bridgeport thought. It was good to see her own beautiful Joan.

11

When Mrs. Bridgeport came downstairs, she found there was nothing much she could actually do to help the situation.

Emily and Charles were out hunting for the cat, and there was nothing to do but wait. Which is often the hardest thing.

Anna made tea, and Mrs. Bridgeport carried her cup to the kitchen window and stood holding the curtain aside with one hand, watching the foggy afternoon grow dark. In the desolate late-winter garden the trees were still bare. Birds had gone early to their nests. Lights glowed at a neighbor's window — a neighbor whose children were all safely home, Mrs. Bridgeport thought.

Finally she sent Joan to look for Charles and Emily, a probably useless gesture. No one even knew which way they had taken.

Joan had not been gone long when Charles and Emily came to the back door with dragging steps and forlorn faces. They had not found Kitty, and tears streamed down Emily's face. Mrs. Bridgeport put her arms around the little girl and tried to comfort her, but it was no use. As fast as Mrs. Bridgeport wiped away a tear, another came.

"Kitty will come back," Mrs. Bridgeport promised with more assurance then she felt. She held Emily close and patted her head.

"Mama, she can't stay outside . . . something will happen to her . . . a dog will eat her up." Emily lifted mournful eyes.

"No, he won't, darling. Now don't cry. Everything will be all right."

Even Anna tried to help. She put her large ruddly face close to Emily's teary cheeks. "Kitty will come back. She wants her supper."

Mrs. Bridgeport gave Anna a grateful glance. But Charles was tugging at her arm. "We looked *everywhere*, Mama."

Mrs. Bridgeport's head throbbed, her whole body felt leaden with defeat.

"I want to look some more," Emily begged. She was still crying. Charles looked drawn and pale. They shouldn't go out again.

"Darling, it's so foggy, you might not even see her."

"Yes, we can, yes, we can." Emily wriggled out from her mother's arms.

By now it was not only foggy, but growing dark. Dark came early on March afternoons.

"I don't think so, darling."

"Yes, we can; yes, we can!" Emily's tears came faster as she pleaded. Her coat, so hastily

81

put on, was a button off all the way down. Her hair hung straggly and limp from the rain.

"I'll go with you."

The voice startled everyone. Wilma stood in the doorway between the dining room and kitchen. No one had heard her coming. She was wearing the brown sweater and brown slacks Mrs. Bridgeport hated. Her hair needed brushing. But there she was.

Light glinted on her glasses as she moved into the room toward the scene of grief.

"I'll go with you," she said again, and Emily looked beseechingly at her mother.

"Oh — I don't know." Mrs. Bridgeport cast about for some help, some decision from somebody other than herself. But everyone was looking at her to decide. To tell the distraught children it was too dark to find Kitty seemed a cruel thing. Mrs. Bridgeport could not do it.

Wilma went to get her coat, and Mrs. Bridgeport let them go, Charles muffled up and coughing, Emily with red eyes puffy from crying. Wilma plodded along beside them as they struggled to see in the failing light.

"Here, Kitty, Kitty, Kitty . . ." Emily's wavering voice seemed to echo long after they were out of sight, and Mrs. Bridgeport turned from the door with a disheartened sigh. It was all so hopeless.

12

The next morning Joan walked to school thoughtfully. Sometimes she met Cissy Allen at the corner of Windsor Drive and Sycamore Street. Today she waited a few minutes, but Cissy did not come, so Joan walked on alone. It was just as well. She had some things to think about.

Everything was so sad at home with Kitty gone. Maybe she would be found, of course, or find her own way home. But what if she didn't? Emily loved her so very much. The whole family loved her. Now maybe they would never see her again.

It seemed as though everything had gone wrong lately — since about the time Wilma came. And Wilma wouldn't miss Kitty. She hadn't loved Kitty as the rest of them had. She told Emily she'd never had a pet. She couldn't know how loving one and losing it could hurt.

And it really was very strange about the kitchen door being open, Joan thought. *Wide* open, Anna had said. What had Kitty thought when she saw that wide-open door? She had always been kept so carefully away from doors.

Hurry out, and close the door before Kitty gets out. How often had Joan heard her mother say that?

How often Joan had said it herself.

When her girl friends were leaving, lingering by the open door, Joan always kept Kitty in her arms so she would not run out.

For all these months since Emily had found Kitty and brought her home, there had never been any problem. And now, just while Wilma was visiting, there was suddenly a wide-open door while Mother was upstairs and Anna had her day off, when nobody was around to pick up Kitty and keep her safe.

Greencourt High School had originally been surrounded by a large lawn and stone benches under elm trees. But new additions had been attached to the original building and slowly eaten up the lawns that had been so charming twenty years before. Now only a thin strip of grass separated the buildings from the street, and there were no more stone benches under elm trees. The new sections were stylish, and some attempt had been made to blend their architecture with the old building. Only one square of grass and trees remained, surrounding a statue of Shakespeare. Before morning classes there were usually groups of students sitting on the statue's base and, in fine weather, lounging on the grass. Even on this chill March morning boys stood with books under their arms, hands in their pockets, while long-haired girls in bright-colored clothes clustered together. A few called to Joan, but she hurried by with a brief wave, intent on her own thoughts.

She went silently from her locker to her first class.

Wilma could have done it, opened the door. There was no other explanation. Wilma was lonely and unattractive and poor. *How she must hate us.* Joan felt her face flush, her heart quicken. That was it, of course. Wilma hated them because they had a nice house and nice clothes. She'd never had a pet. She was probably jealous about that, too. So she opened the door. After that, she probably hoped Charles and Emily would get lost in the fog. She probably didn't really look after them at all when she offered to go out searching with them. *Here, Kitty, Kitty, Kitty.* Emily would dart aside into a yard or driveway, and Wilma would walk on, leaving Emily alone in the fog. It hadn't worked, but it might have.

Joan's fingers trembled as she got out her pen to take notes on the next day's English assignment. The period was almost over, and she had hardly heard a word the teacher said.

And she hardly heard now. She was remembering the brooding expression she sometimes saw on Wilma's face. Wilma always seemed to be secretly watching, plotting behind the thick glasses. Since Wilma had come Charles had been half sick all the time, Mother had headaches, even Anna had been acting funny.

Wilma was making everybody unhappy.

Joan felt a tenseness and anxiety she had not known before flood over her. Why, now that she thought of it, it had been days since she herself had been really happy. She couldn't concentrate on her schoolwork with Wilma around, and she felt an indefinable edginess as each evening passed and the time drew closer and closer to when she would have to lie in the dark, listening to hear if Wilma was asleep.

She would have to talk to her Mother. . . .

"Joan."

The English teacher sat at her desk, pointing the eraser end of a yellow pencil toward Joan.

"I'd like to see you a moment, please."

Joan stood at the teacher's desk, hugging her books. The changing bell had rung. She should be on her way to the physics lab.

"What's happened to your work lately, Joan?"

Miss Bosley's voice wasn't unkind. She regarded Joan with a patient expression.

Joan gazed back helplessly.

"You usually do better than this."

Miss Bosley held up a paper marked C minus.

Joan shifted her books uncomfortably. "I'm sorry, Miss Bosley."

Miss Bosley knew classes were changing, that Joan had another class to get to. She put Joan's paper with other papers on her desk, tapping the edges into line.

"I'm expecting better from you on that test next week."

"Yes, ma'am."

Joan fled into the thronged corridor, embarrassed and dismayed. She had never been called up to a teacher's desk like that before in all her life.

13

The rest of the day dragged by. Joan thought it would never end. She wanted to get home and talk with her mother — and study for that English test. Miss Bosley's voice echoed dully in her mind. *I'm expecting better*

from you on that test next week. The more
Joan thought about the test, the more she felt
her mind emptying out, like a pitcher poked
full of holes, draining away all she had learned
in English class. Maybe she would fail the test
altogether.

At three thirty she hurried along the streets
toward home, hoping to arrive before Charles
and Emily so she would have a few minutes
with her mother alone.

But Charles and Emily had beaten her by
moments, and were in the living room being
questioned about something. Joan stood in the
doorway holding her books and listening with
surprise. Someone had apparently done something naughty. But Charles and Emily were
not naughty.

"I didn't do it, Mama." Emily's voice was
puzzled. She hadn't even taken off her coat
yet. Wisps of hair that Joan had curled up the
night before straggled from a red knit cap.

"Heck, no," Charles said, with some indig-
nation at even being asked. "Why would I
do a dumb thing like that?"

Mrs. Bridgeport was distracted. She looked
flustered, Joan thought — which wasn't like
mother.

"No, I really didn't think you did." Mrs.
Bridgeport patted Emily's arm. "I just
thought — oh, I don't know what I think any-

more." She pressed her forehead. Another headache was coming on.

"What's wrong?"

Mrs. Bridgeport turned and saw Joan in the doorway — and Wilma coming down the stairs past the landing.

"What's wrong? What happened?" Joan glanced over her shoulder at Wilma. Wasn't there something ominous in the fat, impassive face and the glare of light on the eyeglasses?

Wilma came across the hall with a slow tread.

"Someone has marked on the wall." Mrs. Bridgeport motioned to the side of the room.

There, above a low armchair, was a row of four waxy blobs. Joan peered at them curiously, and then went to kneel in the chair to touch the marks with her fingers.

"I didn't do it, Mama," Emily said again. Her fragile voice floated in the air like a sigh.

"I know, dear. But how did it get there? Who would do such a thing?"

"I didn't do it." Wilma's voice was matter-of-fact. She pushed at her glasses and stared at Emily.

"Mama." Emily tugged at her mother's sleeve. "Can I go out and find Kitty?"

Mrs. Bridgeport looked down at the upturned little face.

"Yes, run along . . . but don't go too far. It gets dark early, you know."

"I'm going too." Charles had already forgotten about the marks on the wall as he scrambled past Wilma to follow Emily.

"Ask Anna to come here," Mrs. Bridgeport called after the children, and then she sank down on the sofa . . . the sofa where the white cat liked to sleep.

Anna came from the kitchen to study the marks on the wall. She had never noticed them there before, she said with certainty. Anna knew every nook and cranny in the house.

"I don't think they were here before," Mrs. Bridgeport tried to explain. "They just suddenly seemed to come."

Anna stood with pursed lips, her hands clasped across her ample waist. She seemed about to say something, but turned and went toward the doorway, shaking her head with a slow, emphatic motion. Mrs. Bridgeport heard her muttering, "Something wrong here. . . ."

Something wrong? Oh, yes, indeed, Mrs. Bridgeport thought with a sensation of defeat. But *what*?

When she looked up, Wilma was gone. The girl always came and went unexpectedly, Mrs. Bridgeport realized, now that she thought about it. One moment Wilma would be in a room, by a door, on the stairs — the next moment she would be gone.

"Can I get you anything, Mother?" Joan came to sit on the sofa arm, her head tilted with concern. "You look so tired. Please don't worry. I'm sure we can get the marks off."

Joan wasn't sure at all, but it seemed the most comforting thing to say. It certainly wasn't the time to talk to her mother about all the accusing thoughts and decisions she had come to at school that day.

"No, thank you, sweetheart." Mrs. Bridgeport made an effort not to look tired. "I'm all right, just a little headache."

At last Joan went slowly up the stairs and found Wilma sitting by the bedroom window staring out into the growing twilight. Her head was bent toward the pane in an attitude of patient waiting. Waiting for what? Joan wondered. For Emily and Charles to get lost in the dark?

Joan hesitated at the half-open door. It was her room, and she didn't even want to go in with Wilma there.

"Why are you doing all these things!" she blurted out to the hunched figure at the window. And then, startled at her own daring, she ran away into Emily's room, slamming the door behind her.

She waited a moment, her heart pounding. But Wilma did not call out or come after her. Nothing happened. Joan stood by Emily's ruffled bed and stared vacantly at the bedpost. What if she was wrong? What would Wilma think!

But I'm not wrong. Joan's mouth tightened with determination. *Tomorrow I'll talk to Mother. I WILL.*

Alone in the living room, Mrs. Bridgeport went over the afternoon in her mind.

She had looked up from her reading and seen the four marks on the wall. Why, they were letters, she realized: four letters. She stared, openmouthed, feeling a prickling of cold along her arms. Letters?

No, she was wrong. The more she stared, the more the marks blurred together and faded . . . just as before, that night in Emily's room, when her eyes were strained from reading late.

Only this time they did not fade completely. They were indistinct, no longer letters, just blobs. But they were there, a smeary darkness on the pale-ivory wall. It was not caused by imagination or tired eyes.

She had questioned the children, but she knew they would not mark on the wall with crayon. Wasn't it crayon? Mrs. Bridgeport touched the marks and they felt waxy, somewhat like the waxy stain that had spoiled Charles's science notebook.

Then Anna had come. Anna said the marks were not there before.

Before what? Mrs. Bridgeport thought back. Who else had been in the house that day? Only Mrs. Allen from down the street, Cissy's mother. She had come with a white African violet plant. African violets were her hobby. Her house was full of them, blooming on every windowsill that had a north light.

"You don't look well," Mrs. Allen had said in her well-modulated voice.

"No, really, I'm feeling fine," Mrs. Bridgeport lied.

Mrs. Allen hadn't stayed long. She sat with her coat across the arm of her chair, soft gray kid gloves laid neatly on her lap. Then she left.

No one else had been in the house . . . except Wilma.

Joan got ready for bed that night in an awkward silence. She stayed in the bathroom a long time. She set her hair with deliberate slowness, polished her fingernails, hoping Wilma would be in bed by the time she was finished.

The room was dark, and Joan crept into her own bed without turning on a light.

She lay awake, holding her breath to listen to hear if Wilma was asleep.

After a long time, a stolid voice broke the silence.

"I'm not doing anything."

Joan lay rigid with tenseness. What could she answer? What could she say?

She heard Wilma turning in bed, the soft sound of covers being drawn up closer. And then silence.

14

Joan awoke early in the morning. She sat up in bed stealthily. The alarm had not yet rung and she pressed the knob so it would not ring. The room was dim, but she dressed without turning on a light, moving as quickly and quietly as she could. Wilma was still sleeping, and Joan wanted to get out of the room before she woke.

Or was Wilma only pretending to sleep? Joan couldn't tell. Her fingers fumbled with blouse buttons; the closet door creaked as she reached for her shoes. Wilma did not stir.

Joan gathered up her purse and schoolbooks and closed the bedroom door behind her with a sense of relief. The hall was still dark enough to show the light below Emily's door. But morning was coming, another day was beginning. Joan had made up her mind not to let this day slip by without speaking up.

At her mother's door she hesitated a moment and then knocked softly. *Please be awake, Mother.*

The door opened almost at once, and Mrs. Bridgeport stared at Joan with surprise.

"Darling — is anything wrong?"

"Mother, I just have to talk to you. . . ."

Joan closed the door behind her. "It's about Wilma — oh, I don't know where to begin." She stood clutching her books, appealing to her mother to understand somehow.

"Darling, what *is* it?" Mrs. Bridgeport gazed at the distressed face, heard the breathlessness in Joan's voice. "Here, put your books down." Mrs. Bridgeport took the books from Joan and put them on a table by the door.

"I don't know where to begin," Joan said miserably. "I didn't want to wake you up — "

"You didn't wake me up."

Mrs. Bridgeport put her arm around Joan's shoulder and led her toward a chair at the window. "I've been awake awhile. I've just been sitting here watching it get light." She tried to make her voice casual to put Joan at ease.

What now? she was thinking. But she didn't let her concern show. What would she say if Joan asked why she was awake so early? She hadn't told anyone about the sleeping pills. Last night she had not taken one, and now she felt the jittery fatigue of lack of sleep. But the important thing at the moment was to listen to Joan. Perhaps it would only be some little problem. Were there little problems? Lately all problems seemed big ones.

Mrs. Bridgeport motioned to the chair by the window, but Joan perched on the edge of the bed. As though searching for time to compose her words, she let the shoulder strap of her purse slide down her arm and placed the purse carefully on the floor. Then she put her head back and ran her fingers through her long, shining hair.

"What about Wilma?" Mrs. Bridgeport sat in the chair and folded her hands in her lap. She hoped she looked relaxed and poised.

Joan leaned forward with an imploring motion.

"Oh, Mother — can't you send her home?"

"Home?" Mrs. Bridgeport echoed the word blankly.

"She's been here two weeks. That's long enough."

Mrs. Bridgeport felt her fingers clenching.

"Has something happened? I thought you liked having Wilma here."

"I don't like it." Joan lowered her eyes. It sounded so awful, said straight out like that. "Well, I liked it a little when she first came — but oh, Mother, nothing's the same now. Everything's going wrong."

Mrs. Brigeport felt her fingers clenching harder, but she tried to appear calm.

"It does change things to have company. You miss your room — "

"It's not just that." Joan shook her head. "It's everything, Mother. Everything's going wrong. Charles is half sick all the time, and you have those headaches . . . Kitty's gone . . . oh, everything, Mother."

"But, darling, it's just a coincidence that Charles hasn't been well. That's not Wilma's fault."

Joan wasn't listening. Now that she had begun, the words poured out. "She's jealous of us, Mother, because we have money and a nice house. I have to be so careful what I say all the time. She makes me feel guilty. She makes me embarrassed because we have so much more than she does. And we had Kitty. She told Emily she never had a pet. I bet she was jealous of that too. She left the door open — I know she did; I just know it. And she probably broke Anna's flowerpots. She's been making everyone unhappy — I can't even do my homework right with her in the room. She stares at me, and I don't know what she's thinking. She's *creepy*, Mother."

"Joan . . ." Mrs. Bridgeport started to protest, but Joan rushed on.

"She never says anything. She's always sort of lurking around. She's jealous of us, Mother, I know she is. Sometimes I find things in my closet off the hangers, lying on the floor. I tried to be nice to her, honest I did. I offered to let her wear one of my sweaters if she wanted to, but she just said, 'No, I guess not,' like she hated me for offering. Oh, Mother, just think back, everything was so nice until she came. Even Anna's acting strange."

"How is Anna acting strange?" Mrs. Bridgeport was hypnotized by the flow of words.

"I don't know," Joan gestured helplessly. "Anna's just strange lately. She seems to kind of keep looking over her shoulder when nothing's there — oh, I don't know, I can't explain. She just seems to know something's wrong."

Mrs. Bridgeport remembered Anna and Mrs. Cardalla whispering at the kitchen door. *She will not come in*, Anna had said. *There is something wrong here. Mrs. Cardalla will not come in.*

"Mother, I think Wilma left the door open

so Kitty got out. I think she ruined Charles's notebook. I think she stole my silver ring — "

"Your silver ring?" This was the first time Mrs. Bridgeport had heard of that.

"I didn't want to bother you. At first I thought I just lost it, but now I think she took it."

"Oh, Joan, she wouldn't do that. Think back. When did you see the ring last?"

"Well, I can't remember exactly. But, Mother — "

"Maybe you misplaced it long before Wilma came."

Joan shook her head impatiently. "I can't remember. But, Mother, she pushes my clothes on the floor so they'll be all wrinkled and I can't wear them. I *know* she does, Mother."

The intense outpouring was more than Mrs. Bridgeport could cope with. Before she could weigh one accusation, Joan raced on with another. Perhaps if she had slept well, it would all be easier to reason out.

"Can't you send her home?"

"But, Joan, everything probably has a perfectly logical explanation. I hate to accuse Wilma of anything as mean as letting Kitty out or stealing your ring."

Mrs. Bridgeport hesitated and lowered her eyes. There were so many things Joan didn't even know about: the ticking clock, the footsteps she heard at night, the time Emily's night-light had been off. A hopeless weight of depression settled around Mrs. Bridgeport. Wilma? Wilma was her own sister's daughter.

"She made those marks on the wall just to hurt you because you have a beautiful house and you love it and keep it so nice," Joan pleaded. "Please send her home."

"Mama —" Emily's head appeared around the opening door. She had knocked, but no one had heard.

Mrs. Bridgeport stood up as Emily ran in. "We'll talk about this later, Joan. I'm sure everything will work out."

Emily was listening with lustrous eyes. Her hair was unrolled from the rollers and hung in clumpy curls. She had brought the hair brush. Mrs. Bridgeport took it absentmindedly and began to draw it through the soft, fine hair. Joan gathered up her purse and books. She felt drained, defeated. She had wanted a promise from her mother. But she managed a weak smile as her mother touched her arm and said, "I think it's time for breakfast now."

Emily ran to put the hairbrush away, and they went down the hall past the closed bedroom door where Wilma was still sleeping.

The house was quite light now. Charles was awake, talking to his turtle as he laced his shoes.

In the kitchen below, Anna was making breakfast.

It was almost like old times, Joan thought. But not quite.

When the children had gone to school Mrs. Bridgeport sat in the living room and gazed at the gas-log flames. Once again a steady drizzle of rain dripped at the windows. The March morning closed about the house, damp and dreary.

Can't you send her home? Joan had begged.

Yes, yes, she could. Mrs. Bridgeport felt a surge of resolution. She thought over everything Joan had said, piecing together the jumbled phrases in her memory as well as she could. Joan was right. Everything had gone wrong since Wilma came. Nothing was quite right anymore. Sad things had happened.

A shadow crossed the wall, and Mrs. Bridgeport turned with a start. But there was nothing there. She stared at the wall, but there was surely nothing there. The room was still. Raindrops glistened on the windows and the fire glowed on the hearth.

Mrs. Bridgeport looked at the portrait above the mantel and felt decision shaping in her mind, reasonless and relentless, solid as primal rock. There was no mistaking that something had changed about the painting. There had been a joyful brightness on the canvas, and now the children's smiles looked forced, distorting tired faces as they posed in a room from which the sunlight had faded.

Mrs. Bridgeport felt cold with fury. Somehow Wilma had tampered with the painting. It had to be Wilma. How or when, Mrs. Bridgeport could not imagine — perhaps that morning she had gone to Mrs. Arling's to check the fashion-show programs. But hadn't Anna been in the house then? Mrs. Bridgeport thought back frantically. Well, perhaps Anna had gone out to the store for a few minutes and left Wilma alone in the house. Oh, it didn't matter *when*. Somehow it had been *done*.

Wilma must have made the marks on the wall too. Mrs. Bridgeport was sure of that now. And Wilma had sneaked into Emily's room and turned off the night-light to scare her. And she had opened the door to let Kitty out. And stolen Joan's ring. Everything. How had she hoped to get away with all this in a household where the finger of guilt could point only to her? It was stupid — and outrageous. Mrs. Bridgeport felt her whole body seething with anger that Wilma could have done this when they had all tried to be so good to her.

Mrs. Bridgeport leaned her head back and pressed her fingers against tired eyes and a pounding forehead.

All she wanted was to get Wilma out of the house.

Yet it was a hard thing to face, someone so close in the family not being quite "right."

What could she tell poor Catherine? *Your daughter is not "right...."*

Confusion swept over Mrs. Bridgeport. She dropped her hand from her eyes and gazed at the endless rain.

First things first, she thought.

She would send Wilma home, and later, when she was more composed, she would write to her sister and suggest that Wilma should have some counseling, some "help."

What a dreadful letter that would be, when the time came. There was no way she could write it without shocking and hurting dear Catherine, adding to the mountains of problems the woman already had.

But it would have to be done when the time came.

Mrs. Bridgeport sighed deeply. She felt she had failed. She had wanted to help Wilma, to offer some pleasure and comfort to a girl who had so little. She had made her a dress. She had invited Joan's friends for a luncheon to meet her. She had offered movies, books, car rides.

But now she only wanted to get rid of her.

And she would.

Her hands closed into fists to hold this decision tight.

When she left the living room at last and went upstairs to dress she was startled by her own appearance in the mirror. A drawn, grim face with dark-circled eyes gazed back at her. She touched her hand to her cheek and then quickly drew it down to still her trembling lips. *Next we have Madeleine Bridgeport wearing her green chiffon spring gown.* . . . The announcer's voice from the fashion show was a million years away . . . words spoken of a beautiful woman who was gone.

What a mess I am, Mrs. Bridgeport thought with a sinking heart. What's happened to me?

15

In the room off the kitchen, Anna began to pack her bags. Mrs. Cardalla had said she should leave before it was too late. It had been a hard decision for Anna to reach.

One by one Anna packed the books Mrs. Cardalla had given her: *Apparitions* . . . *Evil Forces Roam the World* . . . *Dead Spirits* . . . Oh, Anna knew about *them*. She had heard their laughter in the house at night. Soft, wicked laughter in the dark night.

She had heard footsteps behind her. But when she looked back no one was there.

It was better to do what Mrs. Cardalla said.

After the books came aprons and thick hosiery, a jar of cold cream, a tin of hairpins. One by one the drawers emptied, the closet grew bare. By and by no one would know anyone had ever used this room.

Do not leave anything behind, Mrs. Cardalla had said.

Anna went doggedly from bureau to suitcase. Soon everything would be gone.

Tell Mrs. Bridgeport to leave too, Mrs. Cardalla had said. *Tell her to leave before it is too late.*

It was nearly eleven o'clock before Mrs. Bridgeport came downstairs again. She had stood at her open closet pushing one hanger after another past her with annoyance. This dress wouldn't do. Not this blouse. Not this skirt. Nothing was right. Finally, with a weary, not-caring resignation, she had chosen black slacks and a green blouse. The blouse had been expensive, but now a button was missing on one cuff.

Green beads and earrings.

When she was dressed she hated the outfit,

and stood rebellious and dissatisfied in front of the mirror. She looked dreadful.

It was the lack of sleep. And all this other awful business.

Her hand was unsteady as she traced each lid with green eyeshadow.

Why am I putting on eyeshadow for a morning at home?

She rouged her cheeks heavily. Nothing helped. The dark circles were still under her eyes. Her skin was drab. Her hair wasn't right.

At last she flung open her bedroom door with false defiance and went along the hall.

Wilma was still sleeping. Irritation that the girl could slumber for half the day mixed in Mrs. Bridgeport's mind with relief that Wilma was not up, lurking silently in corners of rooms or lying with a glazed eye fastened on the television set.

Well, there would not be much more of *that*.

"Anna —" Mrs. Bridgeport pushed open the kitchen door and came to a halt.

Anna was sitting in a chair by the kitchen table. An out-of-style black felt hat was pulled over her gray hair. Her broad hands were folded in her lap in a patient, waiting manner. A black coat lay across another chair. By her side were two suitcases, somewhat the worse for wear, with pocked brass corners and scratched sides.

"Anna?"

Everything else flew from Mrs. Bridgeport's mind. Before she could phrase a question, Anna turned her head with a slow, determined motion.

"I'm leaving, Mrs. Bridgeport."

Mrs. Bridgeport's mouth fell open. The door behind her swung slower, slower, and stopped. The kitchen was spotless. Geraniums bloomed on the windowsill.

Anna rose with stiff, self-conscious motions.

"I'm leaving," she repeated. Her chair scratched on the floor as she stood up. "There is something wrong here. Mrs. Cardalla says I should go."

"Mrs. Cardalla?" Mrs. Bridgeport stared at Anna in bewilderment. What was this? Her world was crumbling and she was alone to face it, to hold back tides too mighty for her slender hand.

"Anna — I don't understand — "

"Evil spirits have come to take this house. I have heard them. They laugh at night in the hallways."

Mrs. Bridgeport listened with disbelief.

"Anna, there are no such things as evil spirits."

"Yes, there are. They want to live here in

this house. They want us to go away and leave this house to them. Mrs. Cardalla says so."

"Mrs. Cardalla, Mrs. Cardalla!" Mrs. Bridgeport gestured with confused impatience.

"Mrs. Cardalla knows," Anna insisted grimly. "This is not a good house anymore. My flowers are broken. The poor cat is gone. The spirits walk here at night. They make the rooms cold and the walls sigh."

The walls sigh! Mrs. Bridgeport was incredulous. Anna's belief in ancient evils and superstitions she felt helpless to combat.

"And there are sounds," Anna said.

"Sounds? What sounds?"

"Doors closing." Anna looked sideways from frightened eyes. "At night, when everyone is asleep, I hear the doors closing. And the laughing."

"Anna — "

She had her coat on now. From a pocket she pulled out a pair of gloves and began to put them on.

"Anna, you can't just *go*."

"You should go too, before it's too late. Mrs. Cardalla says for you to go."

Surfacing from somewhere deep within herself, Mrs. Bridgeport felt a frustrated rage, equal to the rage she had felt toward Wilma. Mrs. Cardalla with her séances and palm readings and other murky shenanigans had meddled with the simple, uneducated mind of the good and cheerful Anna. Did people really believe such things? It was ridiculous, unbelievable.

"Anna, that's nonsense." Mrs. Bridgeport was surprised at the sharp, clear sound of her own voice. "There are no evil spirits here."

And then she felt her voice faltering. It was impossible to say to a servant, "It's only my niece, it's only Wilma — and I'm sending her home." It was family, too close, too personal, too embarrassing to discuss with a servant.

Anna did not seem to notice the fading voice. She was picking up one of the suitcases, her face set.

"You go before it's too late."

Another suitcase. She was headed toward the door.

Mrs. Bridgeport could not believe what she was seeing. Without a moment's notice she was losing a good, dependable housekeeper who had been with her nearly two years. She stretched out a hand as though to draw the woman back, but the black-clothed, funereal figure kept walking toward the door.

"Where — where are you going?"

"To my sister, until I find a new place."

"But this is your place, Anna. I'm going to have the wall painted. Everything will be all right. Anna, wait — "

Anna had set down one of the suitcases to put her hand on the doorknob.

"Anna — listen, please. Let's just say you're taking a couple of weeks vacation." Mrs. Bridgeport went a step closer, her hands held out beseechingly. "You deserve some time off. You're always so good to us, Anna. Take two weeks — take three weeks, Anna. But let me call you then. Everything will be all right, I promise you... Anna?"

The door closed. Anna was gone.

16

The phone call went more easily than Mrs. Bridgeport had hoped.

She could hear the phone ringing, and with the intermittent buzz she had a sense of the rooms, the house into which that sound was going. It had been several years since she had visited Catherine. But she could quite clearly see again the small, worn house, the little children sucking popsicles on a toy-cluttered front porch.

Of course they hadn't stayed overnight. There wasn't room. They had been driving to Springfield to see Lincoln's home and all the sights of the capital; they had spent just the afternoon at Catherine's. . . . Oh, how long ago that seemed! Emily had been only six, sleeping, limp and trustful, on a cushion in the back seat of the car. Charles had clamored for hamburgers at every fast-food stand.

Mrs. Bridgeport heard the receiver lift.

"Catherine? Is that you? Hello! This is Madeleine. . . . I'm sorry to call, but I haven't been feeling well lately and — well (an apologetic laugh) — it's really almost too much for me now, having a guest."

Sunlight glinted on the windows. Mrs. Bridgeport could see it as she talked on the phone. It was a good omen: sunlight after so many dark, rainy days. March was half over. Spring was coming. The sun was shining again. And one day Anna would be back.

"Oh, Catherine, I'm so glad you understand." Mrs. Bridgeport spoke rapidly. "We've enjoyed having Wilma, but I think perhaps it would be better if she came home now. . . Yes, we'll see that she gets to the bus station. . . . I'll call you to let you know what time you can expect her there."

Finally, at the end, Mrs. Bridgeport said, "How are John and the children?"

And Catherine asked about Charles and Emily and Joan.

"They're fine," Mrs. Bridgeport said. But

she tried not to sound too gay or too well. After all, Wilma was going home because she was sick. The thought of Wilma's going home made Mrs. Bridgeport feel better, but she tried to sound sick.

"I'll write soon," she promised.

The words echoed dully around her when she hung up the phone. *I'll write soon.* Oh, Catherine, I wish I didn't have to write at all. But I suppose it's only fair that you know what Wilma has done here.

The house seemed too large and quiet when she hung up the phone. There was no Anna in the kitchen now. There was no dear little white cat on the sofa cushion.

Mrs. Bridgeport felt a moment of panic when she finished her call and had to face the empty house again.

But Wilma would be gone tomorrow, and surely Anna would listen to reason and come back. Everything would be all right again.

Charles would stop coughing. Emily would turn off her night-light. Joan would have her room to herself again. Crocuses would peek out along the side of the house, and lilac bushes would bloom on Windsor Drive.

The next call was to the bus station.

Wilma came downstairs just before noon. She was wearing the new blouse Mrs. Bridge-

port had made for her, and Mrs. Bridgeport
felt a pang of guilt.

"It's Anna's day off," she lied with forced
cheerfulness. "So I'll fix your breakfast. What
would you like?"

Wilma sat at the kitchen table, leaning on
her arms. The expression of her eyes behind
the thick glasses was impossible to read.

"Anything's okay."

Mrs. Bridgeport's head throbbed. She ached
for sleep. Feeling overdressed in the green
blouse and green eyeshadow, she set out a
frying pan and spatula.

"How about an omelet? I'm very good at
them."

"That's fine," Wilma said.

Mrs. Bridgeport yearned for people in the
room. She yearned for Emily and Charles
chattering, for Joan smiling and pushing back
her hair, for Anna, plump and rosy.

"Wilma . . ." Mrs. Bridgeport stirred the
eggs carefully, "I've just talked with your
mother. They miss you at home."

"Yeah, I bet."

"They do," Mrs. Bridgeport insisted.

There was an awkward silence.

"Anyway" — Mrs. Bridgeport slid the omelet onto a plate and buttered a piece of toast
with uneven strokes — "we're so glad you

could come for a visit, but they want you home."

"When?" Wilma didn't pay any attention to the food set in front of her. She was watching Mrs. Bridgeport — beautiful Aunt Madeleine. *If only I could look like her.*

"There's a bus at two this afternoon. You'll be home by eleven tonight, and your father will meet the bus." Mrs. Bridgeport sat down companionably at the table. Already a sense of a burden lightening had come over her, and she smiled hopefully at Wilma. "After you've eaten, you can get your things together and I'll drive you to the station."

It was all so fast, Wilma thought. She hadn't planned to leave so fast. She had thought she had so much more time.

She tried to eat the eggs Aunt Madeleine had cooked. But they were gluey in her mouth, and hard to swallow.

When she went upstairs to pack, she took a last look around the room she had grown to know so well. Bare tree branches, tossed by gusts of March wind, scratched against the windowpane. The television set was silent. The pictures of Joan's friends smiled at her from the frame of the dressing-table mirror.

Good-bye, Wilma, they seemed to say. *Good-bye, Wilma.*

17

Saturday morning, the first morning Wilma was gone, began with bright sunlight. Joan wakened and stretched luxuriously. The twin bed across the room was empty. The blue-and-lavendar quilted spread lay flat. Wilma was gone.

In her room down the hall, Mrs. Bridgeport awoke with a similar sense of relief, a peace of mind disturbed only by the inconvenience of having Anna gone. But Anna would come back. The painter would fix the living-room wall. All would be well.

"Come on, slowpoke." Charles nudged his finger at the lazy turtle. The turtle waddled up to the rock in his watery home and blinked at Charles.

Emily wound down the pink foam-rubber rollers, found her hairbrush, and ran to her mother's room to have her hair brushed. She forgot it was Saturday morning, when Mother slept late.

"That's all right, sweetheart," Mrs. Bridgeport said. Anything was all right today.

But the sunlight faded as the morning

passed. By mid-afternoon a foreboding silence spread across the sky. The light was gone. Charles began to cough again, and Joan wandered aimlessly around the house, unable to settle herself to anything.

"Oh, Emmy, can't you ever put anything away," she fussed at a pile of toys in a living-room chair.

Mrs. Bridgeport watched the graying sky, and her feeling of tenseness returned. Where was the relief she had expected to have now that Wilma was gone? When she heard Charles coughing her nerve ends tingled. *Stop*, she wanted to shout. *She's gone. Stop!*

Emily spilled a glass of milk when she had her afternoon snack. Mrs. Bridgeport's head began to throb as she wiped up the puddle on the kitchen floor. "Emily, I don't know why you can't be more careful." She looked at the little girl's drooping face without compassion. She did it on purpose, Mrs. Bridgeport thought. Why are children so messy!

But after Emily had gone, Mrs. Bridgeport sat at the kitchen table, missing Anna and reproaching herself that such a small thing as spilled milk had made her so irritable.

Emily hadn't spilled the milk on purpose.

But she should have been more careful.

It was wrong to be so cross with her.

No, it wasn't.

Yes, it was.

Mrs. Bridgeport's mind tossed this way and that like branches in a raw wind.

The day grew steadily worse. Rain began to fall. Emily cried because Kitty was lost in the rain.

"She'll get all wet, Mama."

"No, she won't. Emily. She's probably in some nice dry place."

"But why doesn't she come home? Doesn't she miss us?"

For this, Mrs. Bridgeport had no answer.

"Can't we go and look for her?"

"Darling, it's pouring rain."

"I don't care."

By evening Mrs. Bridgeport's nerves were completely on edge. She opened the TV listings and read down from seven o'clock through ten with a sinking feeling. The hours stretched forever before her. The hands on the mantel clock stood at seven fifteen. How soon could she take a sleeping pill and put the whole wretched day behind her?

"Mother." Joan came to stand beside the chair where Mrs. Bridgeport sat. "Can we call Aunt Catherine and see if Wilma is really there?"

Mrs. Bridgeport lifted her head. The TV listings hung limply between her fingers.

"But she must be there, or we would have heard."

Joan sank down on the arm of the chair.

"I know it sounds silly, Mother, but I still feel kind of, well, depressed, like when she was here. I thought I'd feel better but it's like she's still here. Nobody's happy."

"But, Joan, I took her to the station myself."

"Did you actually see her get on the bus?"

"Of course I saw her get on the bus."

Wilma had gone up the bus steps, clutching her ticket. She had waved back through the windows as the bus drove off. Mrs. Bridgeport stood with the March wind whipping her skirt; a flurry of dust and grit whirled up as the bus gained speed.

"She got on the bus," Mrs. Bridgeport repeated. "I don't know what you're getting at, Joan."

Joan's eyes filled with tears.

"I can't help it, Mother. I just wish you'd call Aunt Catherine and see if Wilma is there."

Mrs. Bridgeport looked at Joan a long moment. On the pale, drawn face she could see the same frustration and anxiety she felt herself. But if Wilma wasn't home, where was she?

Feeling foolish and vaguely apprehensive, Mrs. Bridgeport dialed her sister's number.

As she waited for the ring to be answered, Joan hung at her elbow. "If Aunt Catherine says Wilma's there, ask to speak to her *personally*."

"This is ridiculous," Mrs. Bridgeport said.

The receiver lifted at the other end of the line.

Feeling quite foolish by now, Mrs. Bridgeport spoke to her sister. "Catherine? Hello. Just checking to see if Wilma arrived safely last night."

Joan fidgeted, nudging her mother.

"I'm glad to hear that," Mrs. Bridgeport said. She glanced up at Joan, who nodded with an urging look. Mrs. Bridgeport turned back to the phone.

"Could I speak to her, Catherine . . . if it's not too much trouble."

There was a pause. Joan waited impatiently. Mrs. Bridgeport looked up and shrugged to indicate she didn't know whether Wilma was coming to the phone or not. In the background of the phone connection she could hear a blur of voices, little children wrangling, the drone of a television set.

"Oh, hello. Wilma?" Mrs. Bridgeport sent a reassuring glance to Joan. "We were wondering if you had a nice bus ride. Oh, that's good. We're glad you got home all right."

When the receiver clicked back into place,

Joan said, "Are you sure that was really her?"

Mrs. Bridgeport smiled. She was tired. Every move was an effort. A smile was a supreme challenge.

"Yes, darling. It was Wilma. She had a nice bus ride, and she's safely home."

Emily came to stand by Joan. Her face was pinched and exhausted. "Can we have cocoa, Mama?"

"Thanks for calling." Joan brushed a kiss across her mother's cheek and went toward the kitchen with Emily.

"I want marshmallows. . . ." Emily's voice was lost as the kitchen door swung shut.

Mrs. Bridgeport sat a few minutes longer by the telephone. She rearranged the things on her desk, the ivory letter opener, the calendar pad. March was half over now. Good, she thought.

When she went into the dining room Charles had joined Emily and Joan, and the cocoa was ready on a tray. Marshmallows were set into the bottoms of cups. The cocoa was in the blue-and-white cocoa pot, which had been Mrs. Bridgeport's mother's — too good for the children to be fiddling with, but Mrs. Bridgeport was too weary to complain.

She sat at the table and pretended to be calm while Emily's tiny hands lifted the cocoa pot and poured dark chocolate liquid over the marshmallows. The cocoa pot was fragile, antique, valuable. Maybe Emily would drop it. It would break into a million pieces, Mrs. Bridgeport thought. Then she would scream. She could hear her scream flooding through the house, shrill and desperate. Then she would be locked up in a room where no one could hear her screaming.

"I'm next, I'm next." Charles rattled his cup on his saucer. Then his racking cough began again. *Stop*, Mrs. Bridgeport cried silently. *She's gone. Stop!* But Charles didn't stop.

"Mother." Joan was holding a piece of paper. "I found this note on the kitchen cupboard."

The stiff paper crinkled in Mrs. Bridgeport's hands as she took it from Joan. She could tell from Joan's expression that she had read what was written on the paper.

"Oh, Mother, I feel so awful."

Mrs. Bridgeport opened the folded note.

Dear Aunt Madlin,
I had a wonderful time. Thank you for the red dress and the blue blouse and everything. You have a nice house. It is very pretty. I'm sorry we couldn't find the cat. I hope it comes back.

Wilma

121

Mrs. Bridgeport read the note through twice with a feeling of remote sorrow, like someone in a dream.

"Where did you find this?" She looked up at Joan.

Charles was swallowing his marshmallow whole.

"You can't do that," he said to Emily, his face flushed with fever.

"Yes, I can," Emily said fretfully.

"It was in the kitchen," Joan repeated. "It was on the cupboard by the toaster, sort of hidden behind the toaster, like she was too shy to want us to find it until she'd left."

Mrs. Bridgeport was dimly aware that Charles and Emily were fussing about something. She looked across the table without really seeing. "Time for bed, Emily."

"Not yet, Mama."

"Emily." Mrs. Bridgeport's tone was severe.

"But, Mama — "

"*Emily.*"

Emily slid from her chair. Her cocoa was only half finished. Why was Mama so cross?

"You too, Charles."

"I'm not through," Charles argued. He stayed defiantly where he was, but Emily went out to the hall with a mournful air.

A lamp on the hall table cast a dusky glow upon the stairs, and Emily paused at the first

step uncertainly. She could hear the clock ticking on the landing above, softly at first, a
whisper that grew louder and more fierce with
every stroke. The heavy shadow of the clock
cabinet stretched down toward her, distorted,
broad and wide, filling up the whole staircase.

The hands of the clock stood now at ten
minutes to twelve.

Emily gazed up numbly at the gigantic
shadow. She wanted to run, but the shadow
was everywhere. Behind her in the dining
room she heard the voices of the others come
to a stop. No one was talking now. The house
was suddenly silent except for the beat of the
pendulum, which came with a throbbing intensity like the pulse of some giant heart beating in the dark.

"Mama?" Emily's voice trembled in the
shadows.

Mrs. Bridgeport did not hear this faint little
voice calling to her. Her eyes were fastened
upon the four waxy marks that had appeared
upon the dining-room wall. They *were* letters,
clear this time, formed completely, spelling
out the message at last.

SOON

The blows of the clock filled all the house
with a hammering roar. There was a shudder

of light along the wall, like a curtain moving in a faint breeze.

SOON

Wilma was gone . . . and it had not been Wilma, after all.

Epilogue

In early May the lilac bushes bloomed along Windsor Drive. Lacy purple clouds of blossoms were framed against the azure sky. The chill, dreary days of March were gone. The Bridgeport house was for sale.

A couple came to see the house one bright spring afternoon; the wife had come before, and she was eager to show her husband through every room. The real-estate agent wisely left them to themselves. A woman in love with a house was the best salesman. The agent lit up his pipe and lounged by the open front door, enjoying the day.

The carpeting, draperies, and curtains were to go with the house, and the wife led her husband unto the living room with enthusiasm.

"Isn't it perfect! These lovely soft colors,

this marvelous big room. And at such a low price. It's a *steal*, darling."

The thick carpeting hushed their footsteps; sunlight dappled the brick hearth. Although the walls were otherwise bare, one large painting hung above the fireplace; the Bridgeport children looked out upon the room.

"I can see why they didn't take *that*." The husband looked up at the gaunt faces of the three children in the painting. "Rather dreadful, isn't it?"

"We can take that down," the wife agreed at once. "The frame is beautiful, though. We might save that. But never mind that now, just look around. Aren't these draperies exquisite?" She fingered the luminous green silk glistening with gold threads. "Our sofa would look perfect here — the bookcase here — "

"It's strange, though." The husband was puzzled. "Why would anyone want to sell this place so cheap? It's as though she just wanted to get out and sell as fast as she could, like she didn't want anything more to do with the house. Maybe we shouldn't be too hasty, dear. Maybe there are some drawbacks we aren't seeing."

"Drawbacks?" The wife laughed at the thought. "This is one of the most beautiful houses I have ever seen. Just wait until you see the bedrooms and the garden in back."

The husband did not look completely convinced.

"Please don't worry." The wife touched his arm with a coaxing gesture. "Apparently something happened very suddenly and the family had to leave. Oh, I bet I know." Her face lit with sudden inspiration. "The real-estate agent said she was a widow. I bet she's going to marry again, and wanted to settle everything here as quickly as she could. She's not even in town anymore; she's way off in California. To get a few extra thousand dollars probably isn't as important to her as winding up her affairs here and starting her new life. There, that explains it, doesn't it?"

"That might be it." The husband nodded agreeably.

He was a tall, stoop-shouldered man, with hair beginning to gray at the temples. He wanted to please his wife and of course the house did seem perfect. He had children of his own, and it would be pleasant to sit around the fireplace on snowy winter days. He had always liked fireplaces.

"But that picture has to go," he added. He didn't like the sickly look on the children's faces.

"They don't look very happy, do they?" the wife mused. "I hope they'll be happier in their new home." She didn't know the children, or their mother, who had so abruptly put up her house for sale, but she felt a sympathy for them. Be happy in your new home, she thought. Be happy. Smile again. Don't be sad the way this picture is.

Dismissing her somber mood, she turned to her husband with a cheerful glance. "Come along. You haven't see the upstairs yet. The bedrooms are perfect. I've already decided which will be ours, and there's a perfect one for the twins, with more closet space than even the two of them can use!"

"That seems hard to believe," the husband remarked wryly. His twin daughters had enough clothes for six girls, it seemed to him.

He let his wife draw him across the hall toward the wide stairway, and the real-estate agent smiled to himself. The sale was as good as made.

On the landing the couple paused by the grandfather clock.

Except for the portrait in the living room, it was the only thing that had been left behind.

"Isn't this clock beautiful!" the wife exclaimed. "The real-estate agent says it doesn't run. We tried to start it when we were here before. But that's no matter, it can be fixed. And doesn't it look elegant here on the landing!"

"Very elegant." The husband nodded indulgently. He had rather a fondness for grandfather clocks, and he was warming to the house considerably.

Their tour of the bedrooms did not last long. Everything was so suitable for their needs, there was no reason to linger, to haggle, to debate, to find fault. They went from room to room, naming all their children's rooms.

Except for carpeting and curtains, the rooms were bare now. No echo remained of the children's voices that had once filled them. There was a stain on one windowsill where a wet turtle bowl had once made a mark.

As the couple came downstairs again, to complete their pleasure and satisfaction with the afternoon, they heard a soft, steady tick-tock, tick-tock of the clock on the landing. The hands pointed to five o'clock, and the May sun, coming in a dazzling shaft through the stair windows, glistened on the glass door behind which the pendulum swung.

"It works, after all," the wife exclaimed with delight. "See, darling. We don't even need to have it fixed. Now everything is perfect. Aren't we the luckiest people in all the world!"